KU-499-116

DEATH WEARS A STAR

The Tengen brothers planned to make themselves all the law there was in Coffin Creek and the surrounding Cochise County. Then they could plunder the area at will. Behind the tin stars they wore, the brothers were killers, pure and simple . . . But they'd reckoned without Calvin Taylor, former Indian scout turned Wells Fargo agent. Taylor would bring real law and order to the town, even if he had to do it at the point of a gun. The result was an explosion of violence and killing.

Books by Andrew McBride
in the Linford Western Library:

THE ARIZONA KID

0123766342

SPECIAL MESSAGE TO READERS

This book is published under the auspices of

THE ULVERSCROFT FOUNDATION

(registered charity No. 264873 UK)

Established in 1972 to provide funds for research, diagnosis and treatment of eye diseases. Examples of contributions made are: —

A Children's Assessment Unit at Moorfield's Hospital, London.

•

Twin operating theatres at the Western Ophthalmic Hospital, London.

•

A Chair of Ophthalmology at the Royal Australian College of Ophthalmologists.

•

The Ulverscroft Children's Eye Unit at the Great Ormond Street Hospital For Sick Children, London.

You can help further the work of the Foundation by making a donation or leaving a legacy. Every contribution, no matter how small, is received with gratitude. Please write for details to:

THE ULVERSCROFT FOUNDATION,
The Green, Bradgate Road, Anstey,
Leicester LE7 7FU, England.
Telephone: (0116) 236 4325

In Australia write to:
THE ULVERSCROFT FOUNDATION,
c/o The Royal Australian College of Ophthalmologists,
27, Commonwealth Street, Sydney,
N.S.W. 2010.

ANDREW McBRIDE

DEATH WEARS A STAR

WARWICKSHIRE
COUNTY LIBRARY

CONTROL No.

Complete and Unabridged

LINFORD
Leicester

First published in Great Britain in 1996 by
Robert Hale Limited
London

First Linford Edition
published 2001
by arrangement with
Robert Hale Limited
London

The moral right of the author
has been asserted

Copyright © 1996 by Andrew McBride
All rights reserved

British Library CIP Data

McBride, Andrew
    Death wears a star.—Large print ed.—
Linford western library
1. Western stories
2. Large type books
I. Title
823.9′14 [F]

ISBN 0–7089–5963–6

Published by
F. A. Thorpe (Publishing)
Anstey, Leicestershire

Set by Words & Graphics Ltd.
Anstey, Leicestershire
Printed and bound in Great Britain by
T. J. International Ltd., Padstow, Cornwall

This book is printed on acid-free paper

Thanks to the brothers W
for getting me started; to Robert for
the title; and to Clare and Manassas
for the names.

In memory of Frank Waters.

1

The eastbound stage came into the swing station at dusk. The reinsman jammed down the brake lever, spent a minute settling the plunging and snorting team as the coach slewed to a halt in dust. At his side the messenger lifted his sawn-off American Arms 12 gauge shotgun; he trained both barrels of this fearsome weapon on the man standing by the stage station building.

The messenger called, 'That you, Taylor?'

The man he addressed stepped forward, lifting the kerosene lamp in his hand to show his face. He said, 'Pike Sandusky!'

Sandusky rested the shotgun across his knees. He told the reinsman, 'Ash, this is Calvin Taylor. Ash Wilson.'

Wilson shivered and hunched into the fleece-lined collar of his jacket; he blew on his chilled fingers. Far below, shadows had captured the desert; here, 4,000 feet up in the mountains the wind cut like a fleshing knife. A full amber moon was pinned on the sky; they called it the 'Apache moon' in this quarter of southern Arizona.

Taylor strode towards them. Wilson glimpsed the man's face; not yet thirty years old, he judged, yet already something of a legend. Calvin Taylor, the hired gun. The range detective. *The mankiller*.

Taylor addressed the messenger. 'You're kind of nervous with that scattergun, ain't you, Pike?'

Sandusky grounded the shotgun, butt first, on the driver's box beside him. 'This stage gets held up from time to time,' he said. He pulled one wing of his black handlebar moustache. 'Like every other time.'

The sole passenger in the coach pushed aside the canvas flap that served as curtain and windbreak over the vehicle's side and poked out his head.

He asked, 'Do we stop here? I nearly froze coming over those mountains.'

Wilson told him, 'We got to change horses. Go on inside and get yourself a cup of coffee, Schneider.'

A Mexican manned the station. He saw to the horses while his woman gave the travellers black coffee and corn cakes. There were two tables inside the station building; Schneider sat at one table, Wilson, Sandusky and Taylor at the other.

Wilson glanced at Taylor. There were rumours that Taylor had Indian blood but his features had nothing Indian about them; although his hair and moustache were dark, his eyes were as startlingly blue as a Swede's. Women might consider him a handsome man, Wilson supposed. Not a showy dresser; his outfit — canvas jacket, levis, work-boots, plainsman's hat — was strictly functional. He wore only one pistol, a common-or-garden seventeen dollar Colt, butt-forward in the holster on his left hip. Outside he'd been carrying the latest model Winchester rifle.

Sandusky said, 'I've known Taylor here eight, ten years. Back then I was a muleskinner for the army and Taylor was scouting for 'em. Against the Apaches. How are things on the reservation, Taylor?'

Taylor shaped a cigarette. 'Quiet, last time I was up there.'

Wilson scowled. 'Only good Indian's a dead one, I say.' He looked to see if Taylor would react; it was said he was soft on Indians, thought they were human-beings with rights etc. There were even rumours that he'd been a squawman, had lived with an Apache woman. But Taylor seemed too busy fashioning and lighting his smoke, he might not have heard Wilson's remark.

Sandusky declared, 'We don't need Apaches to raise hell. Enough white-skins doing that, here in Cochise County.'

Taylor said, 'That's all been exaggerated, ain't it?'

4

Wilson snorted. 'If it is, how come you got hired by Mister Wells and Mister Fargo? How come they need a — ' Wilson caught his tongue before it ran on too far and he said 'hired gun'. Or even 'hired killer'. There was an awkward silence; Wilson covered the last part of it by coughing into the back of his wrist, swallowing and finishing the sentence with, 'a man like you?'

Taylor gave Wilson a quick look. In the tail of it, for a second, was something that put a coldness in the reinsman's belly. Taylor asked, 'And what kind of man is that, Wilson?'

There was another uncomfortable silence. Sandusky broke it, declaring, 'I'll tell you what's happening down here. The back country's full of smugglers, road agents, greaser bandits, stock thieves. Town's full of sharpers, four-flushers, bunco-artists and assassins. If you been hired to clean up all that, Taylor, you got your work cut out.'

Taylor said, 'I'm only here on Wells Fargo business. Stage coach and mail

5

robbery. Anything else is down to the law.'

'Law?'

'You got law, haven't you? The Tengen brothers?'

'Well, they got something in Coffin Creek, but I don't know if you'd rightly call it law.' Sandusky blew on his fingers. 'Cold haul over them there mountains. My fingers like to froze to the shotgun.'

Taylor said, 'I'll set up on the box if you want, Pike, leastways to the next station.'

Sandusky grinned. 'You is a Christian man, Taylor. Despite all evidence to the contrary.'

* * *

Driver, messenger, passenger and Taylor all climbed aboard the coach, Taylor sitting up on the box with Wilson. The reinsman cracked his whip and the coach rattled out of the swing station yard. Taylor rested the shotgun

6

across his knees, tucked his chin into his chest and plunged his hands deep into the pockets of his canvas jacket. There was the taste of snow in the cut of the wind, cold burned his nose and stung his ears. He felt a film of ice enveloping his skin; tomorrow, on the desert, the sun would be hot enough to crack paint but 4,000 feet higher winter still gripped the mountains.

Wilson didn't talk much, concentrating on manoeuvring his six-horse team along the trail in near total darkness. That suited Taylor. Mountains ran along all horizons in black frozen waves. To their right, the south, the Mule Mountains humped out of the gloom; south of them lay Mexico. To the north-east were the jagged Dragoons, where Cochise once had his stronghold. Cochise, after a long and bloody life had managed to die peacefully in his bed; after that his people, the Chiricahua Apaches, had been pushed on to the reservation, leaving this country empty, up for grabs. First to grab had been a prospector, what the Apaches called a 'rock scratcher', who'd gone into these mountains alone. He'd been warned all he was likely to find was his coffin, the back country still being haunted by parties of homesick Chiricahuas; instead, in spring of 1878, he'd stumbled on the richest veins of silver and gold in Arizona Territory. In the four years since, mining-camps had grown up around his original strikes, and then towns — the most important of which, Coffin Creek, had a population of 6,000. A county — Cochise County — had been organized around these new settlements.

Around midnight a light snow flurry whipped around the coach. Taylor bore it grimly; he hated cold. The coach jounced into the next swing station for a final change of horses in the dimness of the small hours. Sandusky asked Taylor, 'You turning blue yet? Want me to take over?'

Through gritted teeth, Taylor said,

'I'll be all right for a while.'

The coach moved off again. A couple of miles along, the vehicle paused at the top of a steep grade, Sandusky climbed up on the box and Taylor got in the stage. They started rolling once more; it was downhill most of the way now, out of the high country. Within a mile Taylor was beginning to thaw out; he was starting to feel life in his hands again. There was a kerosene lamp inside the coach giving light. Schneider didn't seem interested in sleeping, neither was Taylor. Nor was either man interested in making conversation, except once Schneider said, 'I heard you talking. Did you say the Tengen brothers are the law in Coffin Creek?'

Taylor grunted a yes.

Schneider said, 'That's an unusual name, Tengen.'

Taylor grunted agreement.

Schneider rubbed his chin thoughtfully. 'Where've I heard that name before?'

'Alva Tengen; supposed to be a big-name peace officer, up in Kansas, tamed all them wild cowtowns, Dodge City and such.'

Schneider managed a grunt of his own. 'Last time I was in Dodge it wasn't so damn tame. No, it wasn't there, where was it?' After a pause, Schneider declared, 'Well, only ten miles to Coffin Creek!' and relapsed into silence. He sat with his fist pressed to his mouth, frowning, in a pantomime of someone thinking, presumably trying to remember where he'd first heard the name Tengen.

A horse whickered. Hooves clattered on stones. A voice, out in the darkness, called, 'Whoa, boys!'

Taylor put a hand to the Winchester beside him. He whispered, 'Go flat, Schneider!' and pushed the man in the back of one shoulder. Schneider gave him a frightened look and prostrated himself face down on the floor. Taylor blew out the kerosene lamp. He peeled back a flap of the canvas that covered one side of the vehicle and peered through the slit.

The night was paling into dawn, black turning grey. The coach was in a narrow, high-walled gully, deep in shadow, straining up a grade. Hazy shapes moved on the slope above; horsemen. He glimpsed metal; rifles and pistols in the riders' hands. One of the horsemen called, 'Hold up and nobody'll get hurt!'

The coach juddered to a halt. As the grey light slowly turned pink, Taylor saw there were six horsemen; one man riding downslope towards the coach, four more behind him, bunched together, the most distant up on the ridge, silhouetted there. Some of them wore long dusters, covering their clothing. All of them had gunnysacks over their heads, with eye-holes cut in the sacks. Taylor felt fear, an aching in his stomach. His common sense told him they were just men with their heads covered in cloth, yet their masks made them somehow inhuman, terrible.

From the floor, Schneider whispered, 'Road agents?'

Taylor said, 'Yes.'

The approaching rider shaped out of the gloom. Taylor noticed his horse had a long pale blaze along its forehead, one white sock on its near front hoof. The horseman reined in, and lifted the pistol in his hand. His voice, when it came, was curiously muffled, not just by the mask he wore. He asked, 'Which one of you sons of bitches is Calvin Taylor?'

Because of the corner of the coach, Taylor couldn't see exactly what happened next but he glimpsed Sandusky moving. Pike stood and appeared to lift one hand. The man on the blaze-faced horse fired. The half-darkness was stabbed with muzzle-flame; Sandusky slammed back against the body of the coach. He slumped sideways, hanging half-on, half-off the box; the shotgun fell from his hands and clattered on the trail.

Taylor jammed the butt of the Winchester into his shoulder, aiming for a clear shot at the gunnysacker. In the same instant the coach leapt forward and he was jolted back on to his rump. Maybe Wilson used his whip, maybe the horse bolted, whatever, the stage hurled itself upslope, straight at the ambushers. Two of them fired, the noise of guns deafening between the gully walls. A horse squealed. More guns sounded; the canvas before him thrashed as bullets ripped it. He glimpsed, through the slit in the canvas, a horseman flash past as the gunnysackers scattered out of the path of the charging coach. Taylor braced his back against the seat and took a quick aim. A rider loomed, only a dozen yards away. Taylor fired; the butt of the rifle kicked into his shoulder and he was half-blinded by the muzzle-flash. The horseman reeled in the saddle, then the man was behind him. Other guns sounded and the coach jarred as bullets struck the vehicle's rear.

Looking ahead, Taylor glimpsed the horseman on the ridge. This man spurred his horse forward, plunging downslope, coming at the coach head on. He twisted his rifle to his shoulder and yelled. Taylor fired. The rider pitched sideways, struck on a bed of loose shale and rolled loosely downhill, churning shale as he tumbled. Then he was left behind, the coach struck the ridge and plunged down the far slope.

The road agents didn't pursue the coach; for all that, Wilson let the horses run. They ran for a mile until one of the team — the offside wheeler — dropped dead, grounding the vehicle; the horse had taken a bullet during the ambush.

Taylor and Schneider climbed from the coach.

Sandusky was sprawled across the box. Wilson bent over him.

Taylor said, 'Let's get him in the coach.'

Wilson shook his head. He said tonelessly, 'Ain't no need.'

Taylor leaned one arm against the

side of the coach. 'Pike.'

'Right through the heart, looks like. The son of a bitch could shoot.'

'Pike.'

'Wasn't no need for it. Pike was just about to drop the shotgun. They didn't need to shoot. Pike got a wife and kids in Tucson.'

Taylor walked round to the rear of the vehicle. He took his saddle-roll and pack down from the dicky seat. He said, 'Cut loose the nearside wheeler. Four horses'll get you into town all right.'

Neither of the other men moved so Taylor unhitched the horse himself. He said, 'I hit two of 'em. One bad, for sure.' He still felt afraid, he realized, tight knots cramping his stomach. He felt dizzy and his arms shook slightly. Violence always left him that way. *Violence and Killing.* In his mind's eye he saw the road agent falling from his horse, spinning down the slope, the limp, ragdoll way he fell. *The way a dead man fell.*

Wilson came to life at last; he cut the dead horse loose from the team and rehitched the four remaining horses to the coach. Taylor tried to get a bridle and saddle-blanket on the spare horse but the animal attempted to bite and then kick him. Taylor lost patience. He found a large, dish-shaped rock and cracked the horse on the forehead; the animal staggered, shook its head but stood passively whilst Taylor climbed on its back. Wilson and Schneider were both staring at him; perhaps they were staring at the Apache moccasins he held, thigh-length deerskin boots that he'd draped across the horse's withers; perhaps they were staring at the look on his face.

Schneider asked, 'What are you going to do?'

'Go after them.'

'All six of them?'

Taylor didn't reply. Wilson said, 'We'll get a posse out after you, soon as we get to town. Take one of them waterbags.'

'Obliged, Wilson.' Taylor took a skinbag of water from the rear of the coach. 'The one who shot Pike — remember his horse? Dark horse, blaze face, white sock on the near front hoof. Ain't gonna be many horses around like that.'

Wilson lifted his head, he stared at the body on the driver's box. 'Well, Taylor,' he said, 'welcome to Coffin Creek.'

2

Full light showed Taylor the country: red desert, encircled by a spine of mountains; low brush, mesquite and chaparral, punctuated by saguaro.

Looking over the scene of the ambush, he saw flecks of blood at one place, a large gout at another. Blood he'd spilled. Hoofprints ran south, all in a bunch. After a mile or so, the riders scattered. They'd divided into three pairs, heading south, south-east and south-west respectively. They made no attempt to cover their tracks; it was easier to run as fast as they could for the border, with Mexico only forty miles distant.

Taylor got interested in a set of tracks which could be easy to trail, a horse with a split hoof, one of the pair of riders who had headed due south for the Mule Mountains. But the men he pursued led him into *malpais* — bad country — and he lost the trail on a plain of bare rock.

Just before dusk he found it again.

Twelve hours later he was lying in cover watching the dawn come, the sun pushing up over the mountains. The night turned grey, then greenish, then pink. And a pattern of dark blotches in the gloom below Taylor's hiding place became visible; two horses, legs hobbled, two bedrolls, a head just visible above each blanket. One of these men ought to be standing guard over the other; at the very least they ought to have risen at first light, instead of lying abed. But there was a reason for their carelessness. Five miles back they'd crossed the international borderline, their camping place was five miles deep in Mexico, where they were safe from pursuit by US law; except today Taylor wasn't concerning himself with legal niceties.

What did concern him was the slope below him. It was of loose shale and gravel, impossible to descend quietly without rousing the men in the bedrolls. Taylor would have to circle around and find another way of coming on the camp. It would be a ticklish business at best, taking these men prisoner; most likely they were sleeping with their guns at their sides, weapons they were ready and willing to use. If Taylor was the killer some said he was, he could simply have shot his quarry where they slept. Instead, he skirted round the slope until he found a place where he could descend to ground level relatively silently. It took him ten minutes; by which time he was damp with sweat, the sweat of fear and tension.

It was full light. Taylor inspected the camp and got a nasty shock. One of the bedrolls had been thrown aside; it seemed the occupant had walked off into the brush, perhaps off to the north where there was a little box canyon. Maybe he'd gone to relieve himself. It left Taylor with a dilemma; whether to take the other man prisoner and risk his companion sniping at Taylor from cover; or to wait for the absentee to return and then brace two men skilled in the use of guns.

Taylor decided to go for the former course. He didn't much like the situation but it seemed the least risky option.

Taylor moved into the cover of a few scrubby juniper trees. He lodged himself behind the bole of one fair-sized juniper. He touched the cedar grip of the Colt in his left-side holster, reassuring himself it was there, then lifted the stock of the Winchester to his shoulder, sighting on the occupied bedroll. His head ached. His throat was suddenly fiercely dry. He swallowed and called, 'Hold it!'

The man in the bedroll fired. He must have been lying with a pistol in his hand as he shot through the bottom of his blanket. It was firing blind yet it panicked Taylor into jerking the trigger; his own shot was a clean miss.

The other man sprang to his feet. The blanket tangled his legs, he kicked it free and Taylor shot him through the chest. He was flung backwards as if he weighed nothing, to lie brokenly on the sand.

Taylor rested his face against the trunk of the tree. His arms began to shake. He realized his nerves were shot to hell and he needed to get them under control if he was to come out of this alive, or if he was to take the other man prisoner.

From the brush to the north a voice came, 'Luke! Luke!'

Before he could stop himself, Taylor fired towards the sound of the voice. A shot was fired in return; a rifle shot. Taylor ducked, but the bullet didn't come close.

He decided there was better cover fifty yards off, behind a scatter of rocks and boulders. He ran, a weaving, zigzagging path, bent over. He was almost at the rocks when something struck him a numbing bow on his left foot. He pitched forward, turning in the air, struck on his back. In the tail of his eye he glimpsed a figure rising from cover, a rifle in his hands. Taylor squirmed over, got his rifle to his shoulder. He and the other man fired simultaneously. Both missed. Taylor lifted his rifle again, so did his enemy. Taylor fired first and he saw the man knocked sideways.

Taylor got slowly to his feet. The other man also scrambled upright, standing with one hand pressed to his side, a fair-haired man in a green shirt. Taylor took aim on him but before he could fire the men melted into cover. Taylor noticed green shirt's rifle was lying on the earth. He heard the man making his way over broken ground to the north; but that was into the box canyon, a blind with no way out.

He took a step forward, winced with pain. He saw a bullet had burned across the sole of his foot, the merest graze. Gasping every time the wound hurt him he walked northwards.

Green-shirt's trail was easy to follow. He'd scattered blood all over his tracks, stumbling and falling in various places. Then Taylor glimpsed the man ahead; he was still running, weaving from side to side, slowing, moving drunkenly. As Taylor watched, the man sank to his knees, sat in the dust.

Taylor walked towards him, not hurrying, the Winchester rested across his arms. Green shirt watched him, a pistol in his hand. There was blood all over his shirt now, and his legs. He was a very young man, maybe still in his teens, with only the pale beginnings of a moustache and beard.

Taylor halted, just beyond pistol range. He said, 'Get rid of that pistol.'

The boy asked, 'What happened to Luke?'

'Dead, I figger.'

'Not his week. He got winged in the hold-up.'

'I did that, too.'

'You winged him, and now you killed him. You killed me, too.'

Taylor raised the barrel of the Winchester, he gestured with it. 'Get rid of the pistol, then we'll see how bad you're hurt.'

'You killed me.'

'I don't figger I have. You'll live.'

The boy grinned, showing blood on his teeth. 'Live to see the hangman, you mean? I didn't kill the messenger. We didn't mean to kill him.'

'Who was it killed him?'

Green shirt waved a pistol in his hand; he appeared to be taking an uncertain aim on his pursuer. Taylor called, 'You damn fool. I'm out of range.'

'I know.' The youth grinned again. 'Give my regards to the hangman.' He turned the gun in his hand. Taylor cried, 'Kid, don't be crazy!' and moved forward, but he was too far away to change what happened. The boy put the barrel of the pistol in his mouth, bit down on the metal and pulled the trigger.

3

Taylor rode north, back across the border, into the foothills of the Mule Mountains.

Late in the afternoon he came on a lonely scatter of buildings in the centre of an empty basin. There were corrals with high adobe walls on three sides, half a dozen horses moving behind the fence bars, a well and water tank. The main house was a fair-sized building in the usual style of low, flat-roofed adobes. There was a barn, an open-faced shed probably used as a smithy, another little shack that might serve as a feedstore.

Taylor rode into the yard in front of the main house. He called, 'Hello the house!'

A door opened and a man stood in the doorway. He had a rifle cradled in his arms, which was to be expected.

He moved forward, out of the shadow of the *ramada*, so that Taylor could see his face; a young man in his early twenties with dark hair, and a slim, wide-winged moustache. Taylor was certain he'd never seen this man before, yet there was something familiar about him. Maybe he looked like someone Taylor knew.

The man said, 'Visitors ain't welcome.'

Taylor blinked. Part of the etiquette of this country was that you fed and housed strangers passing through free of charge, for one night at least; it was so much accepted behaviour on the frontier Taylor was almost shocked by the man's rudeness. It was understandable, however, if there were two road agents hiding in the house, or if this man was one of the gunnysackers himself.

The range detective said, 'Then maybe you can direct me to someplace where I might be . . . welcome.'

The other glared. 'Try back the way you came.' He looked to be thinking about the rifle in his hands, which was a Winchester carbine, calibre of .73, maybe thinking of using it. Taylor was wondering what he'd do about that and then another man appeared in the open doorway. He called, 'Calvin Taylor!'

Taylor hadn't heard the voice in four or five years but recognized it immediately. The man walked towards him, but before he came from the shadow of the *ramada*, to where he could be clearly seen, Taylor said, 'Dave McLennan!' He dismounted and he and McLennan shook hands.

The man with the carbine was staring at both of them; Taylor could see now who he resembled. Taylor told Dave, 'I guess this is your brother.' He managed a small smile. 'Pete.'

Pete McLennan didn't smile, his frozen expression became a scowl. Abruptly he turned away and walked back into the house.

Taylor asked, 'What's the matter with him?'

'Easy to forget your manners, living

all alone way out here.'

Which meant that neither McLennan was married. Not that Taylor was surprised. Out here, women were scarce, at least the kind you married, married women were as rare as hens' teeth. But he guessed there was more to Pete's lack of manners than that; he could tell as much from the trouble in Dave's voice.

McLennan said, 'Come in the house.'

As they walked towards the main house, McLennan said, 'You're limping.'

'It ain't nothing.'

Taylor was six feet tall but Dave stood several inches taller, a large, powerful man who carried his bulk well, a handsome man with a serious, weather-browned face. He was about forty, his dark hair frosted with grey at the temples. He looked his age now; for a long time he looked older than his years. He'd shaved off his handlebar moustache, which left his face looking open, a little innocent and gullible. Which wasn't so, Taylor knew; McLennan was an easy-natured man, conscious of his own considerable strength and slow to anger, but he was nobody's fool.

McLennan led Taylor into the main room of the ranch house. He said, 'There's a Mexican cooks for us. I'll get food rustling.'

Taylor gazed around the room admiringly. The interior was in the New Mexican style, with a floor lower than the ground level aside, a low ceiling from which clay bowls of water hung, to help the air cool, Navaho blankets over the earth floor, glass in the windows and a couple of paintings on the wall. There were Indian artifacts on display. Most impressive, though, was the bookshelf; two shelves packed with the works of Shakespeare, Hawthorne, Dickens, Emerson. Dave could always be found with a book in his hand, Taylor remembered, even in the wildest places. It was an unexpected thing they'd found they had in common, a knowledge of literature, passed on from their respective fathers. Except McLennan senior had been a respected and wealthy businessman of the Old South, ruined by the Civil War; Taylor's pa had been a trader and army contractor around frontier posts; he'd fancied himself as a preacher and a Bible shouter when he was in his cups, which was frequently.

Taylor said, 'Looks like you done all right for yourself, Dave.' A lot of men living alone out in the backcountry let themselves go to hell, usually through the business end of a bottle, but McLennan had kept up his standards. For all that, he was troubled, Taylor sensed; he'd never been one to smile much, but he seemed particularly gloomy now.

The range detective asked, 'You still freighting?'

McLennan poured mescal into two tooth-glasses, a full measure for his guest, a small one for himself. He said, 'No. Sold the business, bought this place. Plan to start a ranch here.

I've already investigated buying into cattle.' He passed a glass to Taylor. 'What about you? I hear you're a lawman now.'

'A mankiller you mean? A hired gun?'

'I didn't say that.'

'How long's it been? Five years since' — Taylor drank — 'you saved my life, Dave. Pinned down like I was, those Chiricahua renegades like to had me . . . '

'Taylor.' There was an edge to McLennan's voice when he said the name. 'I'd appreciate it if you didn't say anything about that to Pete. He doesn't know anything about it.'

Taylor was puzzled. As he'd found the best tack at such times was to say nothing and give the other party a chance to say more, he didn't reply but attended to his drink. Dave poured himself another finger of mescal but for a while all he did was stare at his glass. Finally, he said, 'I guess I worry about Pete. Hell, I've always worried about him, him being sixteen years younger than me and all. Since our folks died, I've been more like a father to him than a brother. Naturally, he resents me for that. Maybe I kept him on too tight a rein, now he's swinging the other way.'

'Everybody's a little wild when they're young.'

'No, they aren't. I wasn't. I never had time to be.'

There was another silence. McLennan continued to stare at his glass, then he said, 'Pete's hanging out with a bad crowd. The Hook brothers. You heard of them?'

'A little bit.'

'Joe and Billy Hook. Funny thing is, with them, it's the younger one, Billy, who's sensible. But Joe, he's wild. Takes after his old man, who got himself killed smuggling a while back. That opened my eyes. Until then I'd thought Joe was all right — a bit hot-tempered maybe, just someone who forgot to grow up. But now I hear he's tied in with a gang of smugglers and thieves, road agents and robbers. I believe it, too. Those are the people Pete runs with now.'

'It's none of my business . . . '

'But?'

The range detective shrugged. 'Pete makes his own choices, he's a grown man.'

McLennan looked like he'd argue with that. Instead, he said, 'You want to wash up before we eat?' His tone was neutral but Taylor guessed he was saying the subject was closed. Right now, Pete McLennan wasn't any of Taylor's business; so much was true. He just hoped it stayed that way. In his mind's eye, Taylor saw the boy in the green shirt, biting on the barrel of the pistol; he heard again the sound of the shot.

4

Pete McLennan joined his brother and Taylor for the evening meal. Afterwards, as the men drank coffee and rolled cigarettes, Pete said, 'So you're the great Calvin Taylor.'

Taylor said, 'I get the feeling you don't like me.'

'That's right.'

Dave blinked. 'Pete!'

'What?'

'Taylor's my guest here. I'll remind you, he's also my friend.'

Pete scowled also. 'You used to be more choosy about your friends.'

Taylor shaped a cigarette. 'It's all right, Dave. Maybe we'd better talk this out. Well, what is it, Pete?'

Pete poured himself two fingers of whiskey. He set the tooth-glass on the table before him. Abruptly he asked, 'Just why are you here?'

'Not that it's any of your business, but . . . I'm working for Wells Fargo.'

'I know who you're really working for.'

'Then maybe you'll tell me.'

Pete smiled ruefully. 'That's it. Put on your killing voice. You're the terrible mankiller; you going to shoot me, Taylor? I'll tell you who you're working for: the Tengens. You're another of their hired guns, aren't you?'

'I've never met the gentlemen.'

'Don't need to have met them. They send you an envelope full of money . . . there I go again. You better get ready to pull the trigger, before I say something else insulting. Can't have the great shootist insulted. Give me a mean look, put on your killing voice, then let's get to guns, so you can shoot me. Isn't that your usual style? Only trouble is . . . ' — Pete raised both his hands from the table, turned the palms forward — 'I'm not heeled. I'm not carrying a gun.'

Taylor smiled also. 'Neither am I.'

He poured mescal. 'Like I said, I'm working for Wells Fargo. Right now, I'm looking for the men who killed Pike Sandusky.'

'Pike Sandusky?' Pete stared. He was either genuinely surprised or doing an impressive piece of acting, Taylor decided.

Taylor told the McLennans about the hold-up; he didn't tell them about the two men killed this morning.

Dave said, 'Sandusky was a family man, wasn't he?'

Taylor nodded.

Dave sat, rubbing the tips of his fingers back and forth across his forehead. 'A terrible thing.'

Pete said, 'That was Pike's job, he took his chances.'

His brother said, 'That doesn't excuse the men who killed him. Why didn't you say something sooner, Taylor? If we'd known . . . '

Hooves clattered in the outer darkness, a voice called, 'Hello the house.'

Dave stood, crossed to the doorway

and opened the door a crack. He asked, 'Who's out there?'

A voice Taylor didn't know replied, 'City marshal!'

Pete said, 'Well, well. Speak of the Devil.'

Dave opened the door. He said, 'Come ahead!'

Three horsemen came into the yard. They dismounted and came into the house. The first man through the door was paunchy, clean-shaven, his brown hair hanging to his shoulders. Taylor recognized the stage driver, Ash Wilson.

Two more men came into the house. Wilson told them, 'This is Calvin Taylor. Taylor, meet the city marshal, Levi Tengen. And this is his brother, Alva. Alva and me been deputized, just for this posse.'

The Tengen brothers stood in the yellow light of the kerosene lamp. Levi was the elder brother, pushing forty, putting on a little weight; Alva looked to be in his early thirties. Yet in most respects the brothers were very alike. Both tall men, in black frock coats, they had drooping handlebar moustaches that hid their mouths, taking any softness out of their faces. Both had yellowish hair, intense blue eyes. Two strikingly handsome men, who'd play the devil with women, Taylor guessed; especially Alva.

Levi Tengen said, 'I've heard of you, Taylor.'

'Marshal.'

Dave said, 'Sit down. You want to eat?'

Levi said, 'We can't stop, Dave. We'll take coffee, though.'

Dave went into the kitchen. The newcomers sat at the dining-table.

Alva seemed a highly-strung man; Taylor sensed the tension in him, in the frown across his brow, narrowing his eyes. There was something unnerving in his piercing blue stare. Alva looked at his hands, began to examine his long, pale fingers, seeming to lose interest in everything else. Taylor had seen gamblers carry on like that, always studying their hands, kneading the knuckles and joints.

Something funny was going on between Levi and Pete, Taylor noticed; a game of glancing at the other sidelong, then away when the look was returned. When Pete's eyes moved to Alva, they became harder, malevolence showed in them.

Levi said, 'We've been riding posse for a day and a half. After those road agents. I hear you shot a few of 'em, Taylor. Good work.'

Alva said, 'We need men like you down here, Taylor. The whole county is overrun with desperadoes. Cowboys, they call themselves.'

Pete sighed. 'I can't believe you're still talking this nonsense.'

Levi raised his head. 'What you saying, boy?'

'Most of the cowboys out there are just that — cowboys. So they might get liquored up come payday, raise a little hell in town. It's all in fun. Most

40

of it. There're no organized gangs; no army of desperadoes.'

Alva said, 'Tell that to Pike Sandusky's wife and kids.'

Levi grunted agreement. 'Exactly. If things are so peaceful, who held up the stage yesterday?'

Pete asked, 'What do you want here?'

Alva looked startled by Pete's rudeness but Levi only smiled tolerantly. He said, 'I like you, Pete. I didn't come here to tangle with you.'

'Why then?' Taylor saw there was a flush to Pete's cheeks, he looked to be on the verge of losing his temper.

'Just tell me,' Levi asked, leaning back in his chair, 'where were you, the night before last?'

Pete got to his feet, he said, 'Damn you, Tengen — '

Alva looked up from the inspection of his slender white hands. He put one foot on the chair before him and leaned forward, resting an arm across his upraised knee. The tail of his frock coat rode back on his left hip, and

Taylor saw the long-barrelled pistol holstered there — maybe a Smith and Wesson American .44 — the ivory grip butt forward. At the same moment, Dave came into the room. He carried a tray with a coffee pot on it, and cups and saucers; he set the tray down on the table beside him.

Wilson asked, 'Just where *was* you the night before last, Pete?'

'What's it to you, you tub of guts?'

Dave said, 'Tell them.'

Pete scowled. He looked at Dave as if his brother had betrayed him in some way. After a minute he said, 'At the lineshack. About ten miles west of here.'

Levi nodded. 'Now, that's interesting. You see, that's where we found one of those road agents. Feller named Luther Perkins. Ain't that strange? That's where Luther was, this morning. Name mean anything to you, Pete?'

Taylor asked, 'You got anything out of him yet?'

'Not hardly.' Levi smiled. 'He was

dead, unfortunately. Your handiwork, Taylor?'

The range detective frowned. 'I figgered I'd killed one of 'em.'

'Shot right through the heart, near enough, so it's a mystery how he travelled so far, unless he was taken dead weight, tied to his horse. Maybe. No doubt Luther was the one, though, the one you shot, Taylor. A gunnysack lying by the body. Also the damnedest disguises! A beard made out of unravelled rope sewed on a piece of black cloth. There was even a wig! Maybe those road agents were theatrical types!'

Taylor said, 'The one you really want is the one who killed Pike. He was riding a horse with a blaze face, a white sock on the near front hoof.'

A troubled look crossed Levi's face; Alva's frown deepened. He said, 'Could be a lot of horses like that.'

'No, I don't figger there are.'

Levi still looked uncomfortable, Taylor thought, and wondered at that. The marshal said, 'Well, we can ask around. Nobody here seen a horse like that, have they? Pete?'

Pete shrugged.

Levi asked, 'What about you, Dave?'

Dave frowned. 'No.' He poured coffee for himself. 'No, I haven't seen anything.'

Levi said, 'This Luther Perkins. He used to work for Joe Hook. Sure you don't know him, Pete?'

Wilson declared, 'You and Joe Hook are big friends, ain't you?'

'So?' Some warmth got into Pete's face again; Taylor wondered if there was bad blood between him and Wilson.

The reinsman studied the back of his hands. 'Anyone see you at the lineshack?' When Pete shook his head, Wilson said, 'Then it looks bad for you, Pete — '

Pete lunged towards Wilson. 'You barrel of lard!'

Wilson ducked around the other side of the table, Taylor and Alva came between the two men. In a reasonable voice Alva said, 'Now, Pete, calm down!'

Pete took a wild swing at Wilson, missing, catching Alva glancingly on the chin. Alva, off-balance, staggered backwards, slipped to one knee. Taylor looped both his arms around Pete, pinning his arms to his sides. He held the squirming man a minute, then said, 'All right!'

Alva got to his feet. His gun was in his right hand. Taylor was close to him; he could see no anger in the man's face, except his mouth was closed tight and his nostrils were flared. He said, 'Don't you put your hands on me!' He lifted the weapon until it was level with his face; Taylor saw the long barrel was engraved with scrolls, stars and other designs.

Levi said, 'There's no call for guns, Alva!'

For a second, Taylor was looking into the blue intensity of Alva's eyes; he noticed a nervous tic pulsing in the man's cheek below the right eye. For a second he expected Alva to strike Pete with the barrel of the gun. Then Alva gave a sigh; he lowered the pistol and pushed it back into the holster. He breathed slowly through his nostrils. He said, 'I'm sorry. Nobody puts their hands on me!'

Taylor released his hold on Pete. Pete fixed Alva with a look of pure hatred; he scowled at everybody else in the room.

Wilson said, 'You attacked deputized law officers, Pete, that's — '

Levi said, 'Shut up, Ash.' He tried to smile reasonably, but made a poor job of it. 'Looks like we both got brothers can be hotheaded, Dave.'

Dave said, 'Unless you're arresting Pete, or charging him with something, then maybe you'd better leave.'

That was Dave, Taylor thought; polite always, his voice was neutral, without anger. Yet men like the Tengens listened to him; the lawmen left.

Taylor poured coffee for himself and the others. 'So, those are the Tengens. I'd heard Alva was the head of the clan. That's what it says in the dime novels. But Levi looks to be the brains of the two.'

Dave grunted, an ironic sound. 'So he is. Which is why he's the city marshal and Alva's just a saloon-keeper and faro-dealer; although Levi deputizes him whenever he can.'

'But wasn't Alva a big lawman up in Kansas? Tamed all those wild cowtowns? Made the country a safe place for women and kids?'

Pete snorted. 'That sounds like more of Alva's bullshit. He spins all those wild stories about himself.'

Dave asked, 'What is it, Pete? Between you and the Tengens?'

'Nothing.'

'Oh?' Dave drank coffee. 'I agree with Pete about one thing, Taylor. If you want to find your road agents, don't look amongst the cowboys out in the backcountry. Most cowboys are working too hard to ride the high lines.'

'Where then?'

'If I were you,' Dave said, 'I'd look in Coffin Creek.'

5

Coffin Creek was a straggle of buildings atop a treeless plateau, with the desert lapping about it to the south. To the north the town backed against Apache Peak, a brooding volcanic butte. Ten, or thirty miles distant, in all directions, a spine of mountains ran against the sky.

Calvin Taylor came into town late in the afternoon from the south; he quickly became aware that this end of Coffin Creek was the Mexican quarter. Low, flat-roofed adobes, brush shelters, goats and chickens everywhere. A little further on, the Anglo presence started to assert itself; Taylor came upon houses built from timber, even a few houses with fenced gardens, tiled and peaked roofs. A huge water wagon came towards him; he manoeuvred his horse, a lineback dun he'd bought from the McLennans, out of the path of the vehicle, and the dust it raised in its rear.

He almost backed his horse into a man coming down the street who seemed to have walked into Taylor's dust; this man leaned against a fence, coughing into his handkerchief.

Taylor said, 'I'm sorry, mister — '

The man lifted his face from the handkerchief.

Taylor found he was staring, despite himself. Several things about this man commanded attention. He was well dressed in black frock coat and stringtie but what was particularly unusual about his clothing was the long overcoat he wore on top of everything else; it was a hot day, too hot for a top coat. He was tall and skeletal, his heavy moustache spanning his narrow face, with its sunken cheeks, the grey-blue eyes burning feverishly, far back in his head; eyes brilliant with pain or sickness. Easy to guess the nature of that sickness, if you took note of one more striking feature about him: the colour of his skin. He had the ghastly, grey-white pallor of someone in wound shock. Then you might wonder if the paroxysm of coughing that bent him almost double was caused just by dust getting into his lungs.

As if to confirm Taylor's suspicions, the man started fighting for breath. The hoarse, sucking noises he made set Taylor's teeth on edge. His face had some colour now, but bad colour, purple-crimson that showed like splashes of dried blood on his shrivelled cheeks. With something like horror, Taylor realized that this man wasn't much older than himself; not much past thirty, he guessed, but aged and wasted by his disease.

The man spat on the earth, made a sound of disgust, wiped his lips with the handkerchief. He pushed a strand of very pale, straw-coloured hair out of his eyes and fixed Taylor with a venomous stare. He demanded, 'What are you looking at, you sonofabitch?'

His slurring drawl made him from the Old South, Georgia or Alabama.

'Nothing.'

'Then why don't you — ' The man offered an obscene suggestion.

Taylor kneed his horse gently in the flanks, rode on down the street. He heard the man behind him begin to cough again, but didn't look back.

The town ahead was changing; he was moving into the section where falsefronts reared against the sky, where stores and shopfronts alternated with saloons. The latter seemed to be doing a fair business already; he heard a piano rattling away.

A figure moved out from under an awning advertising General Merchandise, stood in the street just ahead of Taylor. It was Schneider, the passenger from the stagecoach. They greeted each other. From his voice, Taylor guessed Schneider had been trying out some of the saloons for himself.

Schneider said, 'I see you just met one of our leading citizens.'

'Did I?'

'Sure you did. Doctor Henry Zale.'

'He looks like death walking around.'

'They say he was an army sawbones till he was dishonourably discharged for drunkenness. Good friend of our city marshal and his brother. Buy you a drink, Taylor?'

The other man swung down from his horse, he let the reins trail. 'All right.'

Schneider said, 'I still can't remember where I came across Alva Tengen before.'

The other man frowned. 'Something's bothering me.'

Schneider paused at the entrance of the nearest saloon. 'What about? Alva?'

'No.' Taylor rubbed his chin, he gazed back down the street. 'What bothers me . . . is Doc Zale.'

★ ★ ★

The saloon Schneider and Taylor found themselves in was called the

53

Long Branch. It looked clean and prosperous; at the end of the long mahogany bar signs pointed to both the dining-room and pool tables. In the saloon itself was a roulette wheel and several gambling tables, with men already clustered around them. The interior was dim; little of the fierce outside sunlight penetrated and the air was already blue with the smoke of cigars and cigarettes. Over this haze, the painting of a young lady reclining on a couch gazed down; she was wearing an enigmatic smile and nothing else.

Schneider and Taylor drank. The former talked, the liquor had hold of his tongue. Taylor made polite noises but he wasn't really listening. The voice he heard, again and again in his head, was Doc Zale's.

Three men entered the Long Branch. Taylor saw it was none other than the doctor himself and the Tengen brothers. They came over to the range detective's table.

Alva said, 'Doc, this is Calvin Taylor.'

Zale blinked his cold, grey-blue eyes. 'Calvin Taylor.'

Taylor said, 'We've met.'

Zale grunted. His mouth twisted; for a second he looked as if he was about to spit in Taylor's eye. Abruptly he turned away and made his way to a table, joining four or five men involved in a poker hand.

Alva said, 'Don't mind Doc. He takes a while getting used to people.'

Taylor smiled a very little. 'Sure.'

Alva said, 'Buy you a drink, men? I feel I ought to apologize properly for that little unpleasantness over at McLennan's. I've got a temper needs watching I guess.'

Alva showed his teeth, he had a winning smile.

Taylor said, 'All right.'

While Alva was getting the beers, Levi said, 'There's a town ordinance . . . '

Before he could finish, Taylor said, 'Sure, Marshal.' He pushed back the tail of his canvas jacket and lifted the pistol from the holster on his left hip with his left hand. He passed the weapon across the table, and laid it on the baize in front of Levi.

The marshal had been watching with narrowed eyes; he'd followed the movement of the gun all the way. Force of habit, Taylor supposed.

Levi picked up the weapon, slipped it into his pocket. 'You can pick it up from my office when you leave town. Any time you come into town, just check your weapons in at the first livery or saloon, they'll keep it for you. No offence, Taylor; this is one rule for all. Keeping men, liquor and firearms separated is one way a law officer like me gets to grow some more grey hairs.'

Alva brought over the beers. Levi said, 'We've got a fine town here. Might end up being the capital of the territory.'

Taylor said, 'You think so?'

'Sure. It's nearer to Mexico than any

other settlement. The Mexican trade's worth two million dollars a year.'

Alva said, 'Town's growing fast. Once the railroad connects — '

Taylor asked, 'What's this got to do with me?'

Alva sighed. Levi had a pained expression on his face. The two brothers glanced at each other, then Levi said, 'All we're saying is that there's a lot of money in this town, and more coming in every day. Someone in the right position could make his fortune here.'

'If he worked hard enough.'

Alva smiled disdainfully. 'Hard work's for mules. Men like us can make our pile here and never step outside the limits of the law.'

'That's an interesting proposition.'

Levi said, 'No proposition. Just stating facts.'

Taylor asked, 'How are you doing on the men who killed Pike? The man on the blaze-faced horse?'

'You've got to appreciate our situation here. We can only do so much. You know how much money there is lying around to be stolen? Stage coaches carry bullion out of town . . . half a million dollars of bullion comes out of the stamp mills every month, and we have to protect all of that.'

'Except Pike's stage was coming *into* town, not going out of it; it wasn't carrying bullion.'

Alva said, 'The road agents could have thought there was other money on board.'

Taylor shook his head. 'They weren't after money.'

'What then?'

'They were after me. They even asked for me by name. Pike got killed because they thought he was me. Didn't Ash Wilson tell you that?'

Levi said, 'I have to go.' He stood and left the saloon.

Taylor asked Alva, 'You still deputized? Or are you a faro-dealer again?'

Alva reached into one pocket of his jacket, came out with an object in the palm of his hand. It was a dull, six-pointed star with tiny balls at each point. The badge had a simple inscription stamped on it DEPUTY U.S. MARSHAL. He said, 'I've been deputized so often recently, I sometimes forget whether I am or not. I'd better go over to Levi's office and turn this in.' He tossed the badge on his hand. 'How much do you figger this thing weighs?'

Schneider said, 'A lot.'

Alva said, 'This little piece of tin — weighs as much as a man's life. It's like a word — words, principles, this — ' he held the star by one of its points — 'they weigh nothing, yet they're what people live and die by.'

Taylor couldn't think of anything to say to that. In the awkward silence that followed, he let his gaze roam around the saloon. If there was an ordinance against bearing arms in town, he suspected it was being enforced selectively; there was a bulge in the pocket of Doc Zale's jacket that looked about the size of a Colt pistol, and there was a smaller bulge in the pocket of his brocaded waistcoat that was about the size of a Remington Elliot .32, a particularly nasty little hide-away gun.

Schneider asked Alva, 'We haven't met before, have we? I seem to recall your name, sir.'

'I think you have the advantage of me.' To Taylor, Alva said, 'The main problem with law-keeping here is the border. Sixty miles all unfenced, unpoliced, not enough army to patrol it adequately. You can cross it at will from either side. A felon jumps the line and what can we do? If they're still in the country, we'll bring them to justice, I can assure you of that.'

Alva seemed to talk in little speeches, Taylor thought, like a politician giving his prepared quotes to the newspapers. Taylor wondered if Alva had started to believe the stuff he'd read about himself in the dime novels. There was another silence. Schneider began to hum a little tune to himself and his beer. 'The Arkansas Traveller'.

Alva said, 'It concerns me that Pete McLennan can't account for himself during the time of the hold-up.'

Taylor said, 'Dave McLennan's an old friend of mine.'

Alva blinked. 'Nobody's accusing Dave. But Pete's keeping bad company. He says he was in that lineshack, but there's no witnesses, of course — '

Schneider paused in his humming. In a voice thick with drink, he said, 'That's where I heard the name! Marshal, was you ever in Arkansas?'

'I'm not a marshal. I'm just a faro-dealer.'

'Was you ever in Arkansas?'

Alva looked trifle uneasy. 'I don't believe so.'

Schneider smirked foolishly. 'That's where it was. Pole Creek, Arkansas. I was serving on the jury there, and there was this feller due in court. Only he jumped bond, he never showed. His name was Tengen. He'd been indicted for horse-theft.' He laughed.

Taylor gave Schneider a sharp look,

but Alva was still smiling thinly. 'As I said, I never was in Arkansas. Anyway, when was this?'

' '71, '72.'

'Sorry friend, I can't help you. That's when I was buffalo hunting, up in Kansas.'

'Well, Pole Creek's not so far from Kansas, up in the . . . '

Alva's blue eyes got a little glaze over them. He said, 'No, you're mistaken friend.' He stood. He said, 'I'll be seeing you, Taylor,' and walked out of the saloon.

'A strange man,' Schneider observed.

'You know, Schneider, I don't understand how you've lived this long.'

Schneider glared stupidly. 'Come again?'

'You damn near accused Alva Tengen of being a horse-thief. You don't even joke about such things out here. Even if it was true, someone's past is their own business.'

The other man got a sheepish look on his face. 'Nonsense. I never said . . . '

Taylor stood. 'I'm going to ask around the livery stables. See if anybody saw or rented out a dark horse with a blaze face and one white sock.'

'Half the town knows who was riding that horse, night of the hold-up. Only they're too afraid to say.'

'Who?'

Schneider tapped the side of his nose. 'I may be stupid, but I'm not that stupid.'

Taylor grunted, a half-disgusted sound; in the same instant there was a sudden burst of gunfire from the street outside.

6

Alva walked across the street towards Levi's office. He had his smile ready for everyone, tipping his hat to passing ladies, Good day-ing the men. Some of the young ladies he addressed dimpled and blushed and started to pat their hair. There was an election coming up for county sheriff. Alva figured he was in with a good chance and he wasn't going to spoil it by letting these fools know what he really felt about them.

He was almost at the marshal's office when the shots came, a ragged burst of fire, two or three shots. There were women's screams. Alva felt fear and his nerves began to hum; he gazed south down the street. There was another shot. Alva saw the man on the sidewalk ahead of him go down, flat on his face. He saw another man fall, and a third, people toppling left and right before the one bullet. A man driving a spring wagon hauled by two mules yelled and whipped up the team. He stood upright on the driver's seat and jumped from the wagon; the mules veered sideways and the vehicle careered into a grounded wagon at the edge of the road and toppled over on its side, one upraised wheel turning as the mules got into a kicking, braying tangle.

Alva started to feel calmer. He gazed over the backs of the prostrate figures and saw a man sitting in the rapidly emptying street in front of a saloon, a pistol in his hand. The man got slowly to his feet and shouted, 'Where are you, you cheating bastard?' He called the same thing several times. Then he began shouting something else, but Alva had trouble making out the words. The man had a heavy accent; he was from Cornwall, England. The diggings were full of these Cornish miners, men nicknamed 'Cousin Jack'. He was drunk, another reason why the words were hard to understand.

The miner lifted his pistol, swung it around. People scattered off the streets, another woman screamed. Some of those who'd thrown themselves flat crawled into the shelter of buildings along the sidewalk. Alva angled his walk across the street and ducked behind a parked wagon. A man stepped into the same cover behind him. Alva turned and saw someone he knew, Sherman Andersson. Andersson was dressed in city clothes, derby hat, a man with a fair, large-boned Scandinavian face and blond hair. Alva asked, 'What's going on, Sherm?'

'That miner tied on a few too many in the saloon. Got to thinking a feller was cheating him at poker and chased him out on to the street. Now he's taking it out on everybody.'

'Where's Turkey Creek Jack Green?'

'Across the street.'

The miner shouted, 'Where is 'ee, you damn cheater? I'll cut 'ees throat!'

The miner had thinning fair hair. He

wore a red flannel shirt, jeans, heavy ankle-boots. He was a bullet-headed man with almost no neck, small eyes deep-set in the red slab of his face, massive shoulders that made him look almost hunchbacked, with thick, short arms. His nose was broken and he had a long scar on one cheek that might have been an old knife wound.

Andersson said, 'Usually the miners sort it out with fists or knives, but this damn fool got a gun from somewhere.'

Calvin Taylor came and stood alongside them.

The miner fired his pistol; a window collapsed in a peal of glass. He shouted, 'I'll find 'ee, you cheater! I'll cut 'ees throat!'

Alva glanced at Taylor. He said, 'You remember I asked how much a tin star weighs? I'd better take that gun off him before he hurts somebody.' Suddenly Alva realized that was something Alva Tengen in the dime novels might have said; he was acting just like his legend! The thought gave him a curious warmth. Maybe if he acted, just this once, like the hero in a yellow-paper novel, he'd have the county sheriff's job in the bag!

Taylor said, 'You ain't even deputized. That's your brother's job.'

There was more shouting from the Cousin Jack but the words were unintelligible. Alva said, 'No, I'll do it.' It was like he was an actor playing himself, saying lines someone else had written. But this wasn't a scene from a dime novel, there was one difference: Alva was afraid. He was dizzy with fear at the thought of what he was going to do. He felt sweat on the palms of his hands and rubbed them against his pants. Too many policemen had got themselves killed this way, not taking on the real hardcases but gut-shot by a drunken fool, a saddle-tramp with one moment of killing meanness on him . . . Hickock, Ed Masterton, 'Bear River' Tom Smith, they'd all been killed by no-account trash, killed for no reason, a rotten, sordid, meaningless end.

Alva glanced across the street. Another man he knew, Turkey Creek Jack Green, crouched behind a water barrel, ready to cover him from across the way. Taylor said, 'If you take him head on, I'll work around behind him.'

Alva thought about that. It made sense, but that meant sharing the glory with another man; he couldn't let Taylor take the election away from him! Before he realized what he was doing, Alva had stepped out from behind the wagon, out on to the open street.

He walked towards the miner, pacing in a dead straight line. With a sick-making sense of panic, Alva realized he hadn't even bought his gun into play, the Smith and Wesson was still in his right jacket pocket. He was striding towards the villain empty-handed, just like a hero in a dime novel. But dime novel heroes didn't feel real bullets . . .

The miner was swinging the pistol loosely in his hand. As Alva stepped towards him, he moved the barrel until it was wavering an aim on the other man's chest. The miner blinked and glared at Alva, his mouth hung open stupidly.

Alva stood, perhaps twenty paces from the miner. He took one step forward. Nineteen paces between them. Sherman Andersson and Turkey Creek and maybe even Taylor would be covering him but he couldn't see them in the tail of his eye . . . all he could see was the black mouth of the pistol in the drunkard's hand. He felt utterly alone.

He lifted his left hand and held it out, palm upwards. He said, 'Give me the gun, Cousin Jack.'

The miner shouted down the street, 'I'll kill 'ee! Where is 'ee, you damn cheater! I'll kill 'ee!'

'No, you won't, Jack,' said Alva, speaking once again in his new voice, the voice of the dime-novel hero, a voice of reason, with no fear in it. He took three more steps as he spoke. The other man looked confused at these words, Alva kept walking. Eleven paces from the miner he said, 'Enough of this foolishness, now. You're scaring people.'

One person he was scaring was Alva Tengen, fear was a cold, rottenness writhing in his belly, a hand tightening around his throat, a light-headedness that left him almost giddy, for all the calm, the strength in the strange new voice he spoke with . . . it couldn't end this way, it didn't make any sense, but what did make sense? There was no sense in the way Ed Masterton died either, no logic or fairness in how Tom Smith was killed.

The Cornishman hung his head, the pistol dangled in his hand. Alva managed six more paces. As he took the last of these steps, the miner lifted his head, a startled look came into his eyes, alarm at how close Alva had got. He trained his pistol on the other's belly, this time his grip was steady.

Alva still held out his left hand. 'Give me the gun.'

It was very silent, Alva realized, a silence that hurt his ears. No sound in the whole world. The miner stared. He pursed his lips and opened them again. His eyes got a bewildered, hurt look in them that suddenly turned to anger, a wild, not-thinking anger, and Alva waited for the shot. He saw himself doubling forward, hands to his middle, splitting over the terrible pain in his guts, the sordid, senseless death after all, his dreams come to nothing, dying with the dust of the street in his mouth . . . then the Cornishman said, 'I weren't gonna kill nobody. Honest,' in a voice Alva could barely hear.

Alva said, 'Sure.' The miner bowed his head again as if ashamed, and Alva reached forward and took the pistol from his hand.

Sherman Andersson and Jack Green came up to him and stood on either side of the miner. Alva told them, 'Take him over to the gaol.'

They led away their prisoner. Alva crossed the street and leaned against an upright outside a store. He took slow, heavy breaths to clear his head of dizziness, his arms shaking violently.

Taylor said, 'That took guts, Alva. More guts than I've got.'

Alva smiled but the fear he was reacting to twisted the smile into something grotesque. He said, 'The things we live and die for.'

He walked over to the office. People on the street stared at him, as if they wanted to speak to him but couldn't find the words. He saw admiration in their faces, maybe even awe.

He entered the marshal's office. Levi and Zale were there. Levi asked, 'What the hell were you playing at? You could've got youself killed!'

'I had Sherm and Turkey Creek to back me up.'

Zale said, 'It didn't look like it, you goddam fool!'

73

Alva sat on the edge of Levi's desk. 'Maybe I started to believe all that stuff they write about us.' He laughed at his own foolishness.

Zale scowled. 'There's too much at stake for crazy tricks like that!'

'You're wrong, Henry. I figger that little show just won me the election.'

Andersson came from the back room, where the cells were. Alva asked him, 'How's the prisoner?'

'Peaceful as a lamb.'

Alva's eyes glimmered with dislike. 'There's another thing. Feller named Schneider. He knew me at Pole Creek, ten years back. Can you believe that?'

Zale said, 'We'll have to shut him up, then.'

'Now, now, Henry,' Alva said tolerantly. 'No need to over-react. I'll take care of it, quietly.'

Zale snorted. 'You'll take one risk too many, damn you!' He was trembling with anger, Alva could see; but that was Doc for you, the least thing put him in a wild rage.

Levi said, 'Come on, Doc.' He and Zale left the office.

Alva went into the back room. Turkey Creek Jack Green was there. He was a large man dressed for a Wild West show, wearing a broad sombrero, fringed jacket, and a handlebar moustache. In the cell, the Cousin Jack sat on the edge of the bed, staring gloomily at the floor.

Alva said, 'Open the cell.'

Green smiled, his eyes bright with anticipation. He unlocked the barred door and Alva stepped into the cell. He said, 'Hello, Cousin Jack.'

The Cornishman looked up, his eyes bleary, a sheepish look on his face. He stood and said, 'It were drinkin' done it. I never — '

Alva gazed at the man's vacant eyes, the small, petulant mouth in the red face; he remembered the pistol trained on his belly, fear tightening in his stomach, he remembered Schneider's laughter. He lifted his pistol from his jacket pocket and rested the long barrel

75

of the Smith and Wesson in the palm of his hand.

The miner made a helpless gesture with his hand. He said, 'Honest, Marshal, I never — '

Alva struck him with the barrel of the gun. The man staggered, fell back against the cell bars, slithered down them. A patch of blood opened on the left side of his scalp, ran into his sparse, flaxen hair. He stared at Alva, his mouth gaping.

Alva turned. Sherman Andersson came into the room and stood behind Turkey Creek. Alva told these two men, 'There's somebody else you might have to deal with later. Feller named Schneider.'

Green and Andersson both smiled.

Alva gazed at the miner with contempt. 'You're leaving town, friend. But first, before you go . . . here's something to remember us by.'

He stepped out of the cell and let Andersson and Green file past him. The Cornishman grabbed a cell bar, tried to lift himself, then sank back. As Green and Andersson stepped towards him, he darted glances from one man's face to another, his eyes widening with fear when he saw the billy clubs they held in their hands.

7

Next morning, Taylor was out on the desert, once again looking over the sight of the stage hold-up.

He paused to drink from his canteen. It was hot as the hinges of Hell's front gate, even so early in the day. He let his eye cross the country; the mountains like knuckles along every skyline; the desert, fingers of saguaro probing the sky like weird antennae. He guessed he'd spent too much time with the Apaches, in his scouting-for-the-army days he'd grown to love this wild, primitive land. A place like Coffin Creek was too brash, crowded and discordant for him; he wouldn't weep if he never saw a town again. Any town.

A little dust wisped around on the desert to the west, the sort of dust a small party of riders might make. Not taking anything for granted, Taylor got his Winchester from the scabbard on his saddle and waited.

The horsemen came nearer; three Anglos. Taylor saw one of them was Pete McLennan. He had time to inspect the two others as they came closer. Both dressed like run-of-the-mill cowboys, red-haired men who looked like brothers. When the riders reined in before him, and greetings were exchanged, Taylor had already guessed who the strangers were. The older of the two red-haired men said, 'I'm Joe Hook. This is my brother, Billy.'

Billy looked barely out of his teens. He had a pleasant, open face and no beard yet. Joe was about Taylor's age, although there was a tension in his face, a wild look in his eyes, that made him seem older. He wore chin whiskers but no moustache; both Hooks had fair skin; they'd have a lot of problems with the Arizona sun.

Joe asked, 'What are you doing

here, Taylor? I mean here, in Cochise County?'

'Ask Pete. He's got a theory about it.'

'I've heard a lot about you.'

'Oh?' Something about Joe's manner was irking Taylor already; unless he'd woken up this morning full of meanness, looking for some trouble to get into. 'What've you heard?'

'That you're just the kind of man those son-of-a-bitchin' Tengens would hire.' Hook plucked at his red goatee with nervous fingers. 'A squaw-humping, Indian-loving, back-shooting — '

Before he could get into his stride, Taylor said, 'Let's just us get to it, if that's what you're about.'

'I haven't got a pistol.'

'I wasn't talking about guns.'

Hook looked surprised. 'Someone like you — use his bare hands?'

Taylor smiled faintly. 'I heard about you, too, Joe. And your pa.'

Joe's face coloured. 'What you hear?'

'That you're a cow thief just like he

was. That you need killing near as bad as he did.'

Joe's red face got redder. He made a strangled sound in his throat. He lifted his foot from the off-stirrup and threw himself from the saddle, aiming to bear Taylor to the ground. Taylor dodged that. The two men circled about each other, fists raised.

Joe swung a punch. It caught Taylor on the chin, jolted him; Joe followed through with a left that brushed Taylor's ribs, drew a grunt from him. Joe was nearly Taylor's height, with the same reach, but he was wiry, not strong; Taylor guessed that much from the punches he'd taken. When Joe stepped forward to strike again, Taylor caught him flush on the chin with a straight jab. Joe staggered. Taylor landed a second punch, right on top of the first. Joe's legs wavered and he fell to one knee. Some of the heat had been taken out of his face; his eyes were a little unfocused.

He seemed to realize he wasn't going

to win any contest decided by punches alone. He came off one knee in a lunge, arms wide, aiming to tackle the other man to the ground. Taylor elbowed Joe's head aside, spoiling his charge. As the man stumbled past him, Taylor struck him in the back, just above the right hip. Joe gave a cry of pain, and ploughed to his knees in the dust.

Hook said, 'You sonofabitch!'

He got to his feet unsteadily, turned. There was a knife in his hand.

Taylor took one step backwards. Billy called, 'Joe!'

Hook paused. He glanced at his younger brother. In the same moment, Taylor produced his own knife from the sheath on his hip, the bluesteel blade nine inches long. He said, 'Well, let's go to knives, Hook, you got the stomach for it.'

Joe blinked; he paused for a moment, then pushed his knife back into its sheath. Taylor sheathed his own knife.

Joe stepped forward. The look on his face said he knew he was going to lose this fight but he made his hands into fists and raised them. He wasn't a coward, Taylor judged, even if he had no taste for cold steel.

Joe plunged forward, arms wide again. Taylor caught one arm, twisted sideways on to Joe's charge and tripped him. The man pitched headlong, spilling over Taylor's thigh, and fell heavily.

It took him a time to get back on his feet where he stood swaying. As he lifted his fist, Taylor's punch caught him on the chin and he went back on his rump. Very slowly, he stood once more. Taylor knocked him down again. Joe sat, his head bowed. He made two or three attempts to rise and then gave it up. He called, 'Billy!'

'What?'

'Ain't you gonna do nothing? He insulted Pa!' Joe seemed to be using both hands to adjust his jaw.

'Ain't my fight.'

Finally, Joe managed to stand. He glared at his brother. 'If you was more like Pa, you would!'

'If Pa was more like me, then maybe he wouldn't be dead!'

Joe opened his mouth but words seemed to fail him. He walked to his horse, still unsteady on his legs, climbed into the saddle and rode off to the south.

The others spent a minute watching Joe's dust recede. Billy said, 'Taylor.'

'Uh?'

'Maybe Joe's no good, maybe Pa was no good, but Joe's my brother. You understand?'

Taylor grunted a yes.

Billy turned his horse and rode after Joe.

Taylor inspected his grazed knuckles, and rubbed his side where Joe's punch had landed. He thought: brothers. This was all about brothers. The McLennans, the Tengens, the Hooks. Three tight-knit clans of brothers.

Pete said, 'I don't care what you think. I wasn't in on the hold-up, I didn't kill Pike.'

'Let's hope not. I aim to kill the sonofabitch who did.'

Pete smiled thinly. 'Dave'd say your job is to apprehend these villains, not administer justice. That's for the courts, isn't it?'

'Sure.'

Pete rubbed his chin. 'Beats me how someone like my brother ever met up with a rough customer like you.' He spent a minute studying the space between his horse's ears. 'I'll tell you something, might make this business a little clearer.'

'What?'

'The bad blood between me and the Tengens . . . it's got nothing to do with this hold-up business, or whether I run with Joe Hook.'

'Oh?'

'A few months ago, Levi's niece came to town — Millie Tengen. Well, I been . . . seeing her. Levi and Alva found out about it. They leathered her, the bastards. Strapped her back to ribbons. They've always been rough on their women. So that's what I owe those sons of bitches.'

Taylor said, 'Sons of bitches.'

'Uh?'

'I've been called a sonofabitch a few times recently.'

'Doesn't surprise me.'

'For what it's worth, I know you wasn't in on Pike's killing. I think I know who was, now.'

He waited for Pete to ask 'Who?' When the question wasn't forthcoming, Taylor asked Pete, 'You planning to go into town soon?'

'Maybe. Why?'

'Could be the Tengens are after you.'

'So?'

'Dave's one of my oldest friends. He saved my life.'

Pete looked surprised. 'How?'

'It happened right around here. About five years ago. Dave was a muleskinner on an army patrol I was scouting for. Apaches ambushed us, I got pinned under a dead mule. Dave got me clear, under fire all the time.'

'He never said anything.'

'There's lots of things about your brother you don't know.'

'Maybe. But I didn't ask him to give up his life for me . . . ' Taylor heard a younger brother's resentment in Pete's voice. Pete gazed at nothing, there was a hurt, petulant look on his face; presumably he was going over old arguments with Dave in his head. He came from his reverie, gave Taylor a sharp look. He said, 'You're frightened that Dave's going to get sucked into this 'cos of me, that I'll get him killed.'

'Maybe you should both stay out of town a while.' Taylor saw protest building in the younger man's face and said, 'I don't know everything about the Tengens, but I know the kind of men they are. Even if they do make up stuff for the dime novels. Hardcases like them — they'll kill you, Pete.'

Pete sneered, 'I'm not afraid of the likes of them.' He turned his horse and rode off to the south.

8

Alva Tengen was sitting at a table in the Long Branch, dealing cards to himself. He flipped the pasteboards and laid them face up on the green baize, a frown slowly forming around his eyes. Joe Hook entered the saloon, got a whiskey at the bar then crossed to Alva's table.

Alva asked, 'What happened to your face?'

Joe took a drink. 'Horse threw me.'

Tengen studied Joe's face a moment; the nature of his injuries didn't look like those caused by a fall from horseback. But Alva didn't pursue the matter. He said, 'We need to talk.'

'All right.'

'Go round to the rear of the building. I'll see you in the back room, in five minutes.'

Five minutes later, Alva folded up

the cards, slid out from behind the table and left the main room of the saloon. He walked along a narrow corridor, turned left and entered the back room. Joe was there, sitting at a table; he was using both hands to adjust his jaw.

Alva asked, 'Horse throw you on your chin?'

Joe's eyes got hot. Alva said, 'I've got the perfect medicine.' He turned, took a bottle down from the shelf and poured into two tooth-glasses. Standing with his back to Hook, he smiled with contempt. 'Fourteen-year-old bourbon.' He got rid of his smile, turned and handed Joe a glass.

Hook was nervous, chewing at his lower lip and fingering his goatee. 'What do you want, Alva?'

Doc Zale entered. He and Joe exchanged glances, their eyes showing a glimmer of the dislike they felt for each other.

Alva said, 'I hope you two aren't going to start fighting again.'

Zale lifted the bottle, grunted in approval and poured himself a shot. He sank into a chair and lit a stogie then produced his own pack of cards, shuffling, cutting and reshuffling the deck on the table before him.

Alva paced up and down a few times, then sat opposite Joe. He took off his black, wide-brimmed hat and threw it on the table. Then ran his hands through his mane of yellow hair. 'I don't know. You think things are just coming right . . . and then they get all messed up.'

Joe said, 'Well, of course they are.' He glared at Zale. 'Why the hell did you have to kill Pike Sandusky?'

Zale turned up a jack of clubs. 'Son of a bitch made a fight and got left. What was I supposed to do?'

'Pike was well liked. He had a family. Feeling's running pretty high about it.'

Doc inspected his fingernails. 'You're breaking my heart.'

'If you hadn't been drunk — '

'We were out for a killing and you know it. That's why we were there. To kill Taylor. If he hadn't changed places with Pike — '

'If you'd've been sober, you'd've seen it was Pike up there, and not Taylor!'

Alva said, 'Goddammit! Talking about 'what ifs' don't help us. What we do next — that's what's important.' He rubbed his mouth with the back of his hand. 'The election for county sheriff's next month, we need to get things right by then. How many of us in the hold up? You, me, Doc, Luther Perkins   God rest him.'

Zale's thin, bloodless lips twisted with irony. 'It was Taylor rested him.'

Alva continued, 'And Luke and Ira. Where the hell are those two, anyway?'

Doc said, 'Took off for Mexico with Taylor on their heels. Could be they're still running. Maybe they'll stay down there.'

Hook shaped a cigarette. 'I doubt

it. Young Ira's seeing a girl in the Mex quarter. And Luke ain't one for the wild places. Likes the soft life too much. They'll be back here in town, soon enough.'

Alva said, 'That's no damn good.' He pressed his fingers into his forehead. 'One of 'em will talk.'

Joe looked surprised. 'Them boys? They won't talk.'

Alva tugged at the left wingtip of his moustache. 'They'll get liquored up, or . . . Luke always was a damn leaky mouth, anyway. Or Taylor'll get to 'em. No, one of 'em will talk. It's not like before. Not just a hold-up, this time, Pike Sandusky got killed!'

Doc started to have trouble with his breathing. He sucked hoarsely at the air and the sound put a coldness in Alva's belly, deepened the frown he knew was stamped on his brow. One night soon, Zale would be hunting for breath and he wouldn't find any; he'd die then, drowning like a fish jerked up on shore; there'd be no place in whatever scarred, shredded wreckage was left of his lungs for even one more breath.

Alva said, 'I don't like this. But we've got to make sure — we can't risk them talking.'

Joe asked, 'You want to pay them off?'

Tengen glanced at Hook, surprised at how slow he was being; then he saw the look on Joe's face and knew he understood after all, but was reluctant to say it. Zale put it into words. 'Alva means to kill them. There's only one way to guarantee silence.'

Joe said, 'I'm no killer.'

Doc snorted with contempt. 'You were there when Pike got it.'

'I didn't pull the trigger.'

'You were party to it. That's all the law cares about. They'll hang you as quick as me!'

'How about,' Alva said, 'we set up another hold-up? Get Luke and Ira to do it? Only I'll be there, and Levi. Maybe Doc too. Soon as Luke and

Ira show up — well, we shoot them down like the mangy dogs and road agents they are!' Alva laughed. 'We'll be heroes, Luke and Ira'll be shut up and the election'll be in the bag! That's the important thing — the election. I get the county sheriff's job, Levi's city marshal, it means, between us, we're all the law there is in Cochise County!'

Joe said, 'What's that to me?'

Alva smiled. He rarely smiled, open-mouthed, showing his fine teeth; he could transform his face that way, take the austere quality, the harshness, out of it, but it was a weapon he used sparingly. 'We won't forget our friends, Joe.'

'Friends? What about Ira and Luke?'

Zale sneered, 'Honour amongst thieves. How touching.'

Joe's nostrils flared. 'You miserable one-lung bastard — '

Zale's grey face turned white. He pushed himself out of his chair, one hand to the pocket of his overcoat.

Joe stood also, even though he was unarmed.

Alva said, 'What price honour now?'

Hook moved to the door. 'It's a dirty deal. I want nothing to do with it.'

'Think about it.'

Hook left.

There was a long silence. Alva began to inspect his fingers, knead the knuckles. He asked Zale, 'Well, Henry? What do you think?'

'I don't think he'll go along with it. Not even for the money. And even if he does . . . I've never trusted that hill-country trash. Joe's wild. Unreliable. You need stable men around you.'

Zale's words made Alva think. The big job, county sheriff, was almost in his grasp; $40,000 a year in tax collections . . . but more than that. Respectability. Fame. All he'd ever wanted. But was he like Joe — unreliable? Was that why Levi succeeded and he failed, was there some flaw in him that always brought his plans to ruin and always would?

Doc started to cough into his handkerchief. He drank some whiskey to cut that off. 'I'm with you on Ira and Luke. But why stop there?'

Alva frowned. 'Joe, you mean?'

'He can witness against us, can't he? And then there's the McLennans. Dave saw me.'

'He said he didn't. I wonder why?'

Zale shrugged. 'Point is, he can always change his tune. He is another can witness. Maybe we can tie the McLennans in with Joe. Spread word around they're in this together.'

'You think anyone'll believe that? I'd like to get that sonofabitch Pete, mind. He put his hands on Millie.' Alva poured himself another drink. 'And then there's another damn thing. That leaky mouth, Schneider. Still talking up how he knew me in Arkansas, how a Tenger was arrested for horse-theft. Practically told everybody in the Long Branch.'

'We'll have to shut him up, too.'

Alva nodded. 'We can't let anything

spoil this. I'm so close, now, Henry. I've nearly got it — here in my hands.' He lifted his hands, they held an invisible sphere; his fingers were hooked into claws.

9

Calvin Taylor didn't return to Coffin Creek directly. He went to Tucson, the largest town in the territory, seventy-five miles north and west. He was there two weeks. When he returned to Cochise County he called first at the McLennan ranch.

Pete wasn't at home but Dave was. He fed his visitor; afterwards they talked.

Dave clipped the end of a Mexican cigar. He said, 'So you went to Tucson.'

Dave wasn't going to ask any questions directly, Taylor knew; that was against the etiquette of the frontier and Dave's own code of politeness. Taylor ran a cigar under his nose, grunted appreciatively. 'I needed to ask some questions, get some things straight.'

'And did you?'

Taylor smiled. 'Anything happen down here while I been gone?'

McLennan's eyes narrowed. 'Rumours are flying around.'

'Oh?'

'It seems the gangs of wild cowboys terrorizing this county have put the word out. Against the Tengens. And Doc Zale. If the Tengens don't quit town — ' McLennan lifted his hand, drew one finger across the air before his throat, symbolically slashing his windpipe. 'They get it. Death threats have been issued against Levi Tengen, family and associates: the *Coffin Creek Epitaph* reported it all. You know who leads this murderous band?' There was a copy of the *Epitaph* lying on the table. Dave lifted it.

'No.'

'Those noted villains the Hooks and the McLennans.'

Taylor took the cigar from his mouth. 'You, Dave?'

'That's what it says in the paper.'

'Who started these rumours? The Tengens? Why should they turn against you? Just because of this business with Pete and Millie?'

'You know about that, huh?' Dave took a volume down from the bookshelf, turned it in his hands. 'Taylor, when Alva asked me if I'd seen anyone . . . on a blaze-faced horse . . . I lied.'

'Oh?'

'What's more, he knew I'd lied. I saw someone on that horse the morning after the hold-up. And the rider saw me.'

'Who was it?'

Dave opened the book, he studied a page. Taylor saw the book was *Vanity Fair*. He asked, 'Was it Doc Zale?'

McLennan returned the book to the shelf.

Taylor said, 'I met Zale in town. He said my name. He also called me a sonofabitch. Now, he did exactly the same just before he killed Pike Sandusky. I recognized his voice.'

'You sure? Maybe the accent fooled you.'

'No, it was him all right.'

'But you can't prove it.'

'You can, though.' Taylor stared at McLennan. 'Dave . . . someone like you. Strong on the law. Why'd you lie about seeing . . . whoever it was?'

'Because I thought the Tengens might be in on it. And . . . '

'And Pete, too? Well, was he? Is that why the Tengens started talk against you? 'Cos you can both witness against them?'

Dave shrugged.

'When you going to town again?'

'I've got to go in in a few days for supplies. Why? You want me to stay holed-up here, like a criminal? Hide from the Tengens? I haven't done anything.'

'Well, as long as you're armed . . . ' Taylor's voice trailed off as he saw the look on Dave's face.

'I don't carry a handgun, you know that. Anyway, if I'm carrying a gun the

Tengens'll have an excuse to go after me. They can say they're enforcing the law against bearing arms in town.'

'What about Pete?'

'Like you said, he's a grown man. He makes his own choices.' There was a pause, then Dave said, 'Maybe it's you who needs to watch out. You know how men in your line of work end up — '

'Shot dead, you mean?'

'Or kill the wrong man and end up with a rope around your neck.'

Taylor relit his cigar. 'I met Joe Hook.'

'Oh yes. Pete told me.'

'Anybody called Luke in the Hook gang?'

'There's a Luke Harris.' Taylor listened while Dave described Harris. He asked, 'A young feller run with him? A fair-haired boy, starting on a beard, about nineteen?'

'Might be Ira Samuels.'

'What're they like? As people, I mean?'

'Luke's no good. Ira's just a wild kid,

got in bad company. Why'd you ask?'

Taylor frowned. 'No reason.'

★ ★ ★

McLennan and Taylor went outside and looked over the horses in the corral. There were a dozen animals in the saddleband now, most of them of green as a dollar bill.

'There's a few young cowboys help with the horse-breaking,' Dave said. 'Ira Samuels used to. This is going to be a good little horse ranch. We've got water, graze . . . '

Taylor was only half-listening. Mention of Ira had put the frown back on his face. He gazed towards the mountains. This was his favourite time of the day, getting close to dusk, when the land was fire-coloured, the sky mauve, the mountains purplish. He could smell dusk smells: the tang of sage, nopal cactus, the curious fragrance of the earth as it cooled. He saw, in his mind's eye, his Apache woman, dead how long? Eight years? More? How long since he'd last thought of her?

He said, 'You used to lecture me on the importance of real law and order coming out here . . . well, I'm the real law, aren't I?'

'I meant courts and judges.'

'Not mankillers.'

'The law's too big to be left to the judgment of just one man. Too easy for that man to start playing God, cutting corners on the law and making up his own rules.'

'What about when the law comes out like Alva and Levi Tengen?'

'If that's all the law we've got, then we have to abide by it. Maybe even *they* serve some kind of function when times are wild. I mean, they're only acting for the worst of reasons . . . even so, indirectly, they manage to do some good. But afterwards, when real law is established . . . '

'This Luke Harris. I think maybe I killed him.'

Dave blinked. 'What do you mean?'

Briefly, Taylor told McLennan about the killing of the two men the day after the stage hold-up.

Dave asked, 'Why didn't you say anything sooner?'

'I told my . . . employer . . . up in Tucson, the main Wells Fargo man there. Nobody else.'

'Why not?'

'I had my reasons.' After a little pause, Taylor said, 'For one thing . . . I broke some of the rules you were talking about. I went into Mexico, broke international law. I sneaked up on Ira and Luke and before you knew it, both of 'em was dead. I had to kill Luke just about straight off. But afterwards, I thought, what if I'd got on the wrong trail? Come on the wrong camp, jumped two innocent men? Way it worked out, I'd've killed one of them, anyway, even if they were the wrong parties.'

'Well, at least you thought about it afterwards. One time maybe you wouldn't have.'

'When I was younger, I was a mean son of a bitch.' Taylor smiled. 'Some as say I still am. Dave . . . what about Pete? Supposing he was tied in with the Sandusky hold-up?'

'He wasn't. Joe Hook maybe, but not Pete.'

'But supposin' he was tied in with a robbery? Not a killing business, but something he might have to go to gaol for? Would you turn him in?'

Dave pulled a sour face; for a moment he looked tired, a defeated man. He said, 'I'd have to.'

★ ★ ★

Taylor walked his lineback dun into Coffin Creek. It was dark, now, but a full Apache moon was pinned on the sky, silver-plating everything. He entered the settlement from the north. This end of town was still expanding, as the increasing Anglo community threw up more dwellings — timber houses and adobes; some of the newcomers

106

lived in temporary shelters, even the covered wagons they'd arrived in. This tangle of adobes, huts, tents and wagons made a considerable maze, backing on to freight yards, including the big AT corral — the initials stood for Arizona Territory, they were painted in black and white on the sign that hung creaking in the night wind. Off to the north, stamp mills thumped, the mines, the lifeblood of the town, working round the clock. Behind their noise, Taylor heard the off-key rattling of pianos, the distant hum of voices, a scrap of raucous laughter, the saloons, also doing business every hour of the day.

A man walked towards him, following a slightly weaving path. At one point the man stumbled, slipped to one knee. Taylor saw his face in the moonlight. He said, 'Schneider.'

The other said, 'Well, well. The range detective.' From his voice, Taylor guessed he'd been at the bottle again. He said, 'Join me in a drink?'

'I'm tired. I'll see you in the morning.'

Schneider managed a lop-sided grin. 'Give my regards to our noble marshal and his brother. The Pole Creek horse-thief.'

Taylor rode past him, on down the street.

Schneider told the Apache moon, 'Our noble marshal and his brother.' He smirked. He started walking along a narrow path between grounded wagons. A man stepped from behind one of these wagons and stood, facing him.

Schneider halted. He squinted to see the man's face, shadowed by a pulled-down hat brim. It seemed an unusually pale face. Something about it cleared a little of the fuzziness from Schneider's head; unaccountably, he felt a sudden twinge of fear. He took a step nearer the other man, then his sense of fear sharpened. The other wore a gunnysack over his head. Instead of a face there was a white mask, a piece of sacking with eye-holes gouged from the cloth.

Schneider heard a small noise behind him. He started to turn and something struck him hard on the back of the right shoulder. He was knocked forwards, sprawled on his face. He twisted over, crying out with pain as his injured shoulder banged against the earth.

A man stood over him, a billy club in his upraised fist. He wore a gunnysack over his head too.

The blow seemed to have knocked most of the drunkenness out of Schneider's head. When the man with the club stepped forward, Schneider kicked out from the ground. His foot caught his attacker in the stomach. The man grunted and doubled forward. Schneider scrambled to his feet. He saw the other gunnysacker coming at him. This man also held a billy club. He swung the weapon, Schneider dodged and his assailant stumbled past him. Schneider glimpsed an open space, a gap between two wagons and lunged for it. A foot tripped him and he pitched headlong, rolling on to his back. One of the gunnysackers loomed over him, launching a kick at Schneider's head. Schneider grabbed the man's ankle and twisted. His opponent fell heavily. Schneider pushed himself to his feet. But a club caught him on the side of the head; he grunted and fell. After a time, he sat up. The two gunnysackers moved into position on either side of him. In their white masks, in the chill moonlight, they were ghost-like, faceless, inhuman. They stepped closer, lifting their clubs. Schneider lifted an arm across his face and ducked his head into his chest. The clubs came down; the two gunnysackers struck again and again. They paused in their work to exchange a few words and laugh harshly.

10

Next morning, Calvin Taylor heard a commotion on the streets of Coffin Creek. He came out of the boarding-house where he roomed and saw men gathered in front of the marshal's office. He walked over.

The Tengen brothers were helping a man down from the back of his horse. From his clothing, he looked like a *charro*, a Mexican cowboy. The man's left leg was bloody and he gasped with pain as he was lowered to the earth. There was another Mexican cowboy there, literally a boy, perhaps fourteen years old. He was talking excitedly in Spanish. Levi said, 'Take it easy, kid! Talking that fast, I can't follow you! I only got a little cowpen Spanish.'

Taylor said, 'I speak Spanish.' In that language, he asked the boy, 'What happened?'

The boy talked. Taylor listened, frowning. He told the marshal, 'Him and his pa and some others were driving a herd of cattle up from Mexico. They got ambushed in San José Pass. The ambushers run off the herd, killed the boy's pa and the two other *vaqueros* with 'em.'

Levi shook his head. 'Three men murdered!'

Alva asked, 'Who was it?'

Taylor questioned the boy some more. 'He says there was a big man leading them; a man in a blue shirt like an Anglo soldier, with only one eye.'

Levi nodded. 'One eye.'

'You know who he means?'

'Don't know his real name but they just call him One Eye. Might be an army deserter. Heads up a mixed bunch — Anglos, greasers, maybe even some tame Indians. Trash, all of 'em, the worst kind of border scum.'

'The kid figgers they're driving the herd back into Mexico, maybe down through Knife Canyon.' Taylor rubbed his chin. 'I scouted around there back in '77, chasing Chiricahua Apaches. Just happens I know of a trail through the mountains that'll fetch you out at the south end of the canyon, just above the border. Rough going but it'll get you there hours ahead of any other way.'

'So?'

'It might get you there ahead of One Eye. Especially if he's slowed down driving those stolen cattle. There ain't a sweeter place for an ambush than Knife Canyon.'

Alva's eyes gleamed with excitement. He said, 'You're right, by God.'

Two men rode up; Taylor had seen both of them before, hanging around the Tengens. They led two saddled horses and a pack mule.

Alva told Taylor, 'Our deputies: Turkey Creek Jack Green, Sherman Andersson.'

Green said, 'We're ready to go, Alva.'

The Tengens mounted the led horses.

The Mexican boy had some English, he said, 'I go with you! They kill my father!'

Taylor said, 'Go ahead. I can catch up with you in half an hour.'

Levi turned his horse. 'Why? This ain't Wells Fargo business.'

'How else you gonna find that trail?'

Alva said, 'We're obliged, Taylor.'

The Mexican boy climbed aboard his horse. The posse wheeled their animals and rode south out of town.

* * *

Taylor caught up with the others within the hour; six strong, the posse rode on down towards San José Pass. A few miles short of the pass a figure came from cover and staggered towards them. It was another of the *vaqueros*. He'd been cut off from the rest of his companions and his horse had been shot from under him but apart from a few bruises, he was unhurt. He'd assumed that all the rest of the trail crew had been killed in the ambush.

Sherman Andersson sneered, 'Each one of these greasers thinks he's the only one survived. I bet we find none of 'em got a scratch, they was all too busy running!'

Andersson was wrong. Just inside the pass, they found the boy's father. As far as Taylor could tell, the man had been shot in the thigh, then the ambushers had ridden up to him and finished him off. He'd been shot through the back, four or five times, at such close range powder had burnt the back of his shirt. One of the killers had prised a gold tooth from the dead man's mouth with a knife.

The Mexican boy stared, trembling. He began to sob convulsively, bowed in the saddle.

Taylor told him, 'There's no time for tears! That's your father there, murdered! Get your gun and get to work!'

The boy stared at Taylor with hatred. He lifted an arm and wiped his eyes

115

and stopped crying. He glared at his father's body a second more, then he whirled his horse and galloped off.

Taylor said, 'I'll show you that trail.' He rode off after the boy.

Andersson and Green followed but the Tengen brothers rested their horses a minute. Levi stared at the body of the old Mexican, a thin, grey-bearded man. He thought, unaccountably, of his own father and his own childhood.

Alva said, 'That Schneider. Sherm and Turkey Creek took care of him. He should just be waking up about now in some back alley.'

Levi didn't reply and Alva went on, 'We settle One Eye, get the cattle back and nothing can stop us winning the election!'

Levi said, 'You take a lot for granted, Alva. What if we stop a bullet in this fracas?'

Alva smiled a twisted smile. 'Well, in that dust and confusion anyone can stop a bullet ... ' He gazed after Taylor. 'Maybe even Mister

Wells Fargo. Perished nobly in the apprehension of those cow thieves.'

'Kill Taylor?'

'Best way. If we'd done the job properly, three weeks back, we'd've saved ourselves a lot of trouble.'

'I dunno if it was ever a good idea, killing a Wells Fargo man . . . '

'Well, Levi,' Alva said in a reasonable voice, 'you don't want to do it, fine.' He lifted his Smith and Wesson from the holster, studied the engravings on the long barrel. 'I'm not so squeamish.'

'You've got big plans.'

'Big plans for both of us, Levi! Let's go!'

Levi let his eye rest a moment on the still form in the dust, then he kicked his horse into movement.

★ ★ ★

Calvin Taylor got the job of stoppering up the south end of Knife Canyon, keeping One Eye's gang from getting out of the narrow pass and fleeing

117

across the border. He waited in cover now, lodged behind a fair-sized boulder, his Winchester in his hands.

Behind him his dun horse stood, ground-hitched, nose tied with a rag so it wouldn't whinny and alert other horses. Other riders in this vicinity were likely to be One Eye and his motley band of thieves and killers. The horse hung its head showing the wear and tear of the mountain trail they'd followed getting here . . . but at least they'd reached the canyon ahead of their quarry.

It was about half an hour to dusk, Taylor judged, they had that much shooting light left . . . providing, of course, One Eye did come this way after all. The rest of the posse were scattered along the sides of the canyon floor, where they could get their enemies in a crossfire, as long as everyone kept their nerve.

Nerve. That was the main thing. It took that, waiting, as the hours stretched and crawled by, lying there in readiness to kill, to take human life. Taylor had bad memories of that and this place. The Apaches had jumped the army patrol he was scouting for just here, five years back. There were some who'd blamed Taylor for leading the soldiers into that trap, but ambush was the risk you ran when you took on the best guerrilla fighters in the world, in some of the best terrain for ambushers in the world . . .

He blinked his tired eyes and squinted and saw movement ahead of him, a ripple of dust in the heart of the canyon. After a few minutes' study he identified a small herd of cattle, the tiny figure of horsemen flanking them.

It was possible, he supposed, that this was another cow outfit, entirely innocent herders going about their lawful business. They'd know soon enough. The likelihood, however, was that this was One Eye and that business was due to be conducted with guns.

He heard the distant bawling of the

cattle and wiped sweat from his hands, resting his Winchester across the top of the boulder shielding him, hunched forward. The business of guns . . . he remembered Apache rifles barking from these canyon walls, mules and horses screaming, the yelling of the Apaches . . . he was pinned under a fallen mule, the wounded animal braying crazily, lashing out with its iron-shod hooves and Dave McLennan was running to help him, whilst Chiricahua bullets spumed the dust around him, sang venomously past his ears . . .

There was the sound of a shot. Taylor jumped at that, startled from his day-dream, and pulled the buttplate of the Winchester into his shoulder, squinting along the barrel. The cattle had been dawdling along, now they ran. They poured down the canyon, a long stream of dust, growing horned heads and running legs, hooves a dull thunder between the canyon walls, he glimpsed the greys and duns and splashed brown-on-whites of the longhorns flashing through the dust, the horsemen galloping alongside. He heard the grunting of cattle, yells, the spiteful cracking of guns.

One of the riders was hit. He fell sideways amongst the herd. Taylor glimpsed the riderless horse veer aside, then three more horsemen broke from the dust, cutting across the front of the stampede, coming towards his hiding place. Taylor glimpsed a patch of blue that might be the shirt of a US soldier. Taylor fired at the nearest man and missed, but perhaps another rifleman tallied. The horse reared screaming, the rider clinging to the saddle and the herd boiled up behind them, a dark, horned wave crashed against man and horse. The horse reared over backwards, was lost to sight. Taylor thought he heard the man's scream.

One horseman rode directly at Taylor. He glimpsed a wide sombrero, a chest crossed with cartridge belts. The rider fired the pistol in his hand. A second horseman loomed behind him and

Taylor glimpsed the rider's blue shirt. Taylor fired. Blue shirt flopped back in the saddle, bounced against his horse's rump. He somersaulted slowly backwards. Taylor fired at the rider in the sombrero and missed, by which time the man was almost upon him. Taylor fired again and saw the horse go down; the rider pitchforked over the falling animal's head, rolling, fetching up almost at the boulder where Taylor crouched. Taylor sighted on the fallen man, squeezed the trigger and the hammer came down on an empty chamber!

The man in the sombrero got to his knees. Taylor forgetting the pistol in his belt, took his Winchester by the barrel and leapt from the rocks. He sprang downslope, yelling, swinging the rifle like a club. His enemy dodged, lifting a knee and catching Taylor in the stomach. Taylor doubled forward, half-winded, went to his knees, dropping the rifle. The man kicked at his head but Taylor grabbed the Mexican's boot and twisted and the man fell away. The Mexican scrambled to his feet and Taylor hit him with a looping right to the chin and was struck in return. They exchanged more punches and Taylor was knocked back on to his rump; it occurred to him that he'd met his match here. He stood, groggily. He glimpsed blue shirt sitting up a few yards away, one hand to his bloody side. The Mexican sprang at Taylor, who swung a wild punch. It caught the other on the point of the chin and jolted him, toppling him backwards. The range detective bent and grabbed the Winchester at his feet by the barrel. The Mexican stood and again he sprang at Taylor. Taylor swung the rifle, the butt met the Mexican half-way through his leap and knocked him half around. He ploughed to his knees in dust and lay twisted on his side.

Taylor swung around, facing blue shirt. The man was on his feet, swaying. He had his pistol raised, squinting his one good eye, the other was covered in a cloth patch. Taylor heard a shot and One Eye staggered and fell to his knees. His pistol slipped from his hand, and he pitched forward in the limp, ragdoll way a dead man falls.

Taylor turned and saw two horsemen riding slowly towards him, ghost-like in the thinning dust. Alva and Levi Tengen. Levi held a Winchester which he lowered. Alva didn't appear to have a gun in his hand, then he reached into his jacket pocket and produced the Smith and Wesson.

Taylor said, 'I'm beholden, Levi.'

'Uh?'

'Looks like you got One Eye.'

The brothers glanced at each other. Taylor turned away from them and inspected the fallen men. He heard the unconscious Mexican groan. Taylor stepped towards him, moving stiffly, realizing how much the fight had taken out of him. He said, 'This was a tough son of a — ' as someone struck him across the side of the head, above the right ear. He pitched forward, hearing the sound of the shot as he fell.

Sometime later he heard voices. His skull was a cathedral in which a huge bell tolled, each peal booming, shattering; his head was full of noise and pain. He managed to push himself up on his hands, but then his arms sank into the earth beneath him and he slid back into darkness, face first. The voices he heard grew clearer and he made out words . . . a voice he recognized but couldn't identify said, 'Let's kill the sonofabitch! That's what we should've done before!' Later, someone replied, 'No . . . find out what he knows.'

But what did he know? Did he even know his own name?

He felt hands lifting him. He heard more voices, but they made an unintelligible bleariness in his ears, sounds that faded as his senses faded . . .

11

It was a small adobe building, a square room maybe six yards by six. There was a steerhide door. Against the far wall, chains had been hammered into the wall, the chains ending in metal cuffs clamped around Calvin Taylor's wrists. Taylor pulled on the chains, but he couldn't find any strength; the pain in his head was too fierce, draining him. He sat back against the wall.

The steerhide door swung open and a man stood in the entrance. He was a dark shape against the harsh outside glare. Taylor blinked against it. He recognised Ash Wilson.

Wilson said, 'Surprised?'

Taylor said, 'No.' He could barely hear his own voice over the noise in his head, the sound of pain.

'Oh?'

'For a while Wells Fargo thought

you might be tipping off road agents about which stages to hit. Maybe you got word about me coming down here through to them. After all, it was me they were after.'

Wilson said, 'They shouldn't have shot. They shouldn't have shot. They should've seen it was Pike up there, and not you.'

'Why didn't they?'

'Nobody should've shot Pike. That wasn't part of the plan.'

'Something to think about, Wilson, when they put the rope around your neck.'

Wilson frowned. 'Maybe.' He gazed around the bare interior of the adobe. 'Get used to this place. You'll be here for a few days.'

'And then what?'

'Don't know who they used to chain up here. Might've been a military establishment, some sort of army camp; this is where they chained up their prisoners.'

Taylor wondered how far they were

from Coffin Creek. If he hadn't been unconscious, he'd been on the edge of it, in a grey delirium. He had no idea how many hours, or even days, he'd been in that state. The bullet had grooved a trough above his right ear; his skull could even be fractured. He had no idea where he was. There were no window-holes in the adobe, so he couldn't even tell the time of day.

He said, 'If you let me go, Wilson, before this goes any further . . . '

Wilson smiled bitterly. 'Not a chance. Maybe you're right, Taylor. Could be this is all going bad, and the end of it'll be a rope around my neck. On the other hand maybe it won't, and I'll have a lot of things to help me forget about poor old Pike and his widow and kids.'

Taylor decided the pain in his head was so bad he was going to vomit, and maybe faint too. Unconsciousness would be a mercy, at least. He said, 'Lots of money, you mean?'

'Sure. What do you kill for, Taylor? Like you killed Luther Perkins? 'Cos

128

you want to make this country a safer place?' Wilson sneered, 'You pull a trigger 'cos you like doing it. And the money. Ain't that the truth?'

'Which son of a bitch shot me? Alva?'

Wilson stood by the doorway, chewing one thick thumbnail. 'You'll be here a couple of days, I figger.'

'Why? You keeping me out of the way of something? What?'

The reinsman began chewing on his other thumbnail; he started a low, tuneless whistling.

12

Levi Tengen sat at his desk in the city marshal's office. He stroked one side of his long moustache and gazed into a space just beyond the edge of the table. He rubbed his stomach absently; the little breakfast he'd eaten that morning hadn't settled. He'd had a snort of good whiskey on top of the food but it hadn't helped.

Alva came into the office. He'd eaten a full breakfast, looked in excellent spirits. He said, 'Joe Hook and Pete McLennan are in town.'

'What about Dave?'

'No.'

'Let's don't start the shooting, Alva.' Levi heard the defeat in his voice.

'What's the matter?'

Levi didn't answer. After a moment Alva said, 'It's right here, Levi. Now. We've just got to keep steady.'

'And then what?'

'Then it's all ours.'

Levi made a steeple of his hands, putting his fingertips into his mouth. 'I don't know. It never came to killing before. It could all go bad on us.'

'Not if we stay steady. Then it'll come right. Right as it's ever been. We'll have everything we want after today.'

'If only Doc hadn't shot Sandusky . . . ' Levi let his words trail off. Zale was cold-blooded as a snake; he had nothing left inside him but hate, hatred of the world that played a cruel trick on him, ruining his lungs and taking away his full span of years, leaving him with only a short time to take his revenge on whoever he could, on everyone in the world including himself. The only person he ever seemed to give one thought to was Alva. There was something hounddog about him and Alva; the doc followed him around like a stray out of the rain . . .

Levi had a wife at home. That was

the difference between his brother and himself. Having a woman he loved made him cautious as he had so much more to lose. But Alva was free, and that made him fearless. He'd had women in plenty, right now he was squiring a young actress working in one of the town's more respectable theatres, yet none of them ever seemed important to him, he always left them behind. There was even the minister's daughter . . .

Levi said, 'What was her name, that minister's daughter, the one you was squiring, back in Dodge?'

'What?'

Levi laughed. 'Jesus, I'll never forget that! There you was — passing yourself off as a church deacon! Walking up and down the aisle at collection time wearing your gunbelt on the outside of your coat!'

'What are you talking about?'

'And all the time you and the good reverend's daughter . . . '

'Levi, never mind that. What's

important is now! Today! Are you with me or not?'

Levi steepled his hands again, chewed one fingertip. 'I don't know, Alva. We have to settle with Joe and Dave McLennan. Ira and Luke. Then there's Taylor . . . '

'Soon as this business is finished here in town, we take care of him.'

'But where does it stop, Alva? We might have to take Pete McLennan and Billy Hook, too.'

'What choice have we got?' Alva paced up and down a few times. He stopped and glared at his brother. 'All those years, Levi. All those saloons, all those deadfall towns. Never knowing when you'd stop a bullet. And for what? A town policeman's pay? Whores' fines? What you could fleece out of some drunken cowboy? There's a lot more here, Levi, all we have to do is grab it!'

Alva continued to stare at Levi; the other man studied the top of his desk. Alva asked, 'Well?'

After a minute, Levi stood. He took his gunbelt down from the shelf. He smiled. 'Just made sure I go with my boots off.'

The beginning of a frown touched Alva's face. 'It'll be Joe Hook and his crowd who're finished.'

'Sure.'

'After today.'

'Sure, Alva.' Levi buckled the cartridge belt around his waist.

★ ★ ★

It was going to be a hot day, the white noon sunlight bleached Coffin Creek. When Joe Hook came into the Long Branch, his pale-blue shieldfront shirt was starting to feel harsh with sweat under the armpits. His face was red with heat. He cut the dust with a drink at the bar, then went into the dining-room adjoining the saloon. He stood at the counter, studying the lunches available. Someone moved into the line behind him. Joe turned, expecting Pete

McLennan, who was following him up from the corral; instead he saw Doc Zale.

He said, 'Zale.'

'By God, Hook.' Zale's lips twisted in his narrow, ash-grey face. 'This thing between you and me — it's waited long enough!'

Slowly, Joe moved his hands away from his sides. 'You can't back me into anything, Zale. I'm not heeled.'

Zale's washed-out eyes got a strange half-light in them. Joe could see the man's thin arms were trembling and, from a few paces away, he smelt the whiskey on Zale's breath.

Zale said, 'Then you are a god-damned, yellow-spined coward.' The trembling took his body, ran over him like fever chills. The pistol on his right hip was one of the new model double-action Colts. He had the gun slung on a quick-fire rig, which was a slotted belt, no holster encasing the weapon. A mankiller's toy.

Joe looked at Zale's right hand, the

fingertips trembling near the grip of the pistol, then glanced into the man's pale eyes. Zale began to curse him, using a vocabulary gathered from around soldiers, muleskinners, frontier saloons. Joe listened and did nothing; Zale looked just crazy enough to pull the trigger on an unarmed man. He waited until Doc got short of breath and started to cough into his handkerchief, then he moved towards the door.

Zale wiped his mouth, said, 'Get yourself heeled, then. Next time I see you, I might not bother to look if you're armed. Maybe I'll just go to guns!'

Joe nodded. Out front of the building he leaned on a hitching rail, staring slit-eyed into the noon glare. His arms began to shake and he felt the sting of tears in his eyes. Tears of anger. He remembered how frightened he'd been, dry-mouthed with it, staring into Zale's empty eyes. Suddenly he remembered he had a weapon after all, a pistol left in his saddle-roll in the AT corral.

Pete McLennan left the AT corral, looking for Joe Hook. A hundred yards up the main street, he met Alva Tengen. Alva was dressed in black broadcloth and ought to be wilting in the midday heat; but he looked instead, bright-eyed, alert, purposeful, as if he'd resolved some issue that was chewing at him, had come to some sort of conclusion that left him at ease with himself. Pete didn't know if he cared for the look on Alva's face. His unease deepened as he saw how Alva put himself deliberately in the other man's way.

Pete halted. He saw Alva wasn't wearing a gunbelt, but he might have a pistol in the pocket of his long coat.

Pete asked, 'What do you want?'

He was right about the pistol; Alva started to lift his Smith and Wesson from his right-hand pocket, then paused with just the grip showing. He asked, 'Are you heeled or not?'

'No. What's it to you?'

'I'm not a faro-dealer today. I've been deputized.'

'Why?'

A couple of townsfolk wandered past. Alva raised his voice slightly, as he said, 'You sons of bitches have made threats against us. So, next time we meet you'd better be armed.' Alva took a quick look to make sure the passers-by had overheard him then he drew the pistol and held it at his side.

Pete said, 'What threats? I'm not looking for any trouble. I told you, I'm not armed.'

Pete put both hands into his pockets. Alva lifted his pistol and struck him on the head with the long barrel of the Smith and Wesson. Pete staggered and went back on his rump. He lifted one hand to his scalp. There was blood there. Pete looked at his hand, said, 'You sonofabitch!'

Alva said, 'You've made your threats, now get yourself a gun!'

'You yellow, gutless bastard!'

Pete attempted to rise, slipped to one knee. Alva showed his teeth in a smile. He said, 'That's for Millie.'

Pete shook his head, trying to clear it of dizziness. He saw Alva's face change, the man's eyes focused on something. He wasn't looking at Pete, but past him, and he was still smiling. Twisting around, Pete saw two riders coming into town from the north, making for the AT corral. Even at a distance he recognized his brother Dave; Billy Hook was with him.

★ ★ ★

Alva entered the Long Branch. Levi leaned against the bar, nursing a glass of mescal and tugging one corner of his moustache. Doc Zale sat at a table, dealing out cards on the baize, taking drinks from a tooth-glass. The bottle at his elbow was already half empty.

Alva glanced across the room. There were only a couple of other drinkers present at the far end of the saloon;

they wouldn't overhear. He said, 'Guess what? They're all together, up by the main corral. The Hooks and the McLennans.'

'Obliging of them,' Doc said thickly. 'Now we can settle the sons of bitches all together.'

Alva said, 'Henry, I thought today you might just stay sober!'

'But, Alva, you know I shoot better drunk.'

The Tengens didn't smile at the joke. Alva gazed at Levi. 'Well, we're not going to get a better chance than this. Let's go now! If we're lucky we can box 'em in the AT corral! Well, Levi?'

Levi drank; he placed the tooth-glass carefully on the polished bar. 'Just get someone to take off my boots.'

'Stop that talk! This is the day things start going right!'

Levi nodded. He said wearily, 'Remember this: Joe's the one we need to get. Anyone else is extra. But it's useless if we don't get Joe.'

Zale said, 'You can leave him to me.'

Levi glanced at Zale doubtfully. 'Still be four against three.'

Alva smiled. 'That'll make it look better. Four desperate killers against three gallant custodians of the law! Anyway, probably only Pete'll be armed. Even if the rest get guns, only Joe's any kind of hand at this sort of thing. They're not mankillers.'

'Even so . . .'

Zale folded up his deck of cards, slid the pack into his coat pocket. 'Maybe we'd better stop over at your office, Levi, pick up a little extra insurance.'

Levi nodded. His face, Alva noticed, was pale.

Doc asked, 'Are me and Alva deputized?'

Levi said, 'As of right now.'

Doc drank his whiskey, coughed into his handkerchief. He stood and took up his brass-headed cane. 'We'd better pick up those damn tin stars, too.'

Levi nodded. Together the three men walked from the saloon.

13

Dave McLennan and Billy Hook stopped off on their way to the AT corral to buy tobacco. Coming out of the store, Dave saw Alva Tengen on the sidewalk. Alva had Dave's horse by the bit and seemed to be inspecting the animal's teeth.

Dave asked, 'What are you doing?'

Alva gazed at him strangely; there was a slightly wild look in the man's eyes. He smiled but there was something crazy in that smile, also. He said, 'Another McLennan.' He studied Dave and McLennan knew he was looking for a gun.

'What do you want?'

Alva jerked the horse's head up. Unaccountably, Dave felt a surge of temper. He said, 'Take your hands off my horse!'

That strange stare again. Alva said,

'Keep him off the sidewalk then. He's blocking the road.'

Which was obviously untrue, Dave could see, but he said nothing. Alva, still smiling, walked back into town.

Dave found his arms were trembling slightly and he realized he was afraid. Why?

Billy came out of the store and he and Dave mounted their horses and rode to the AT corral. As they dismounted there, Joe Hook came towards them.

Billy asked, 'Where're you going, Joe?'

'I'm going to get out my saddle-roll.'

'Why?'

Dave said, 'That'll just give the Tengens an excuse to come after you. I just met Alva and he's looking for trouble; why give him any?'

Joe spat into the dirt. 'I thought Zale was going to pull on me a while back. Even though he knew I wasn't heeled. I think him and the Tengens intend to murder me.'

'I've got a better idea than you getting your gun.'

'What?'

'Go and get our supplies someplace else.'

Joe looked startled. 'Dave? You mean let them run us out of town?'

Dave breathed heavily and took his time replying. 'The better part of valour, and all that.'

Pete approached. He asked, 'Where're you boys going?'

Dave said, 'Back the way we came.' He noticed a gash on Pete's forehead, above the right eye. Blood was newly dried about the gash, a bruise was already darkening there. 'What happened to you?'

Pete's lips trembled with anger. 'Alva Tengen. He buffaloed me. Even though he knew I wasn't heeled. Waited until my hands were in my pockets, then hit me with his gun.'

Joe said, 'By God, Dave, you think we should stand for this?'

For a minute Dave felt nothing but

anger too. He saw Pete had a pistol holstered on his left hip, the cedar grip of the Colt turned forward. 'I thought you said you weren't heeled.'

'I wasn't. But after Alva hit me, I got my pistol out of the corral. Next time I run into him I'll be ready, he won't buffalo me again!'

Joe said, 'I'm with you, Pete! I'll get my gun, too!'

Dave said, 'That's what he wants, can't you see?'

'I don't intend to let that goddam tinhorn push me around.'

Dave leaned forward and gripped Joe's left arm gently. 'Joe, listen. It's obvious the Tengens are out to push us into a fight. Why let them? They'll just say the law's on their side.'

Billy said, 'He's right, Joe. We're being set up.'

Nobody spoke for a minute. Then Joe said, 'All right, what do we do?'

Dave said, 'Ride away, leave them to it.'

Pete glared. 'Run, you mean?' He

145

gazed at his brother, and asked, 'Are you afraid, Dave?'

After a moment Dave said, 'Maybe.' The word didn't taste as harsh in his mouth as he'd imagined.

He could tell Pete was looking to Joe for some kind of lead and was surprised when Joe said, 'Let's go. When we settle with the Tengens, we'll choose the time and place.'

Pete opened his mouth to protest. Joe didn't wait for that, but walked into the corner of the corral where his horse stood. He took the horse by the reins and led it towards the corral entrance, where the heavy sign creaked as it swung. Dave got his own horse and followed; Billy ditto. As he passed out of the yard, under the AT sign, Dave saw Pete was bringing up the rear, leading his own horse. Dave felt a smile, with some relief in it, form on his face.

He expected Joe, leading the file, to turn right, which would have put them on the north road out of town, but instead, Joe turned left, making for a sidestreet just past the newspaper building, that would put them on the west road, and a quicker route home. They led their horses past the first of three buildings that hemmed in a backlot, Jones's camera shop and photograph gallery. Suddenly Joe halted and Dave almost walked into the back of his horse. Joe said, 'Look.'

Dave gazed south down the street, his eyes narrowed against the two o'clock glare, his skin pricking from the heat of the sun. He made out three men approaching. He knew two of them were the Tengens, though he couldn't make out their faces, and between them was a man as tall as the brothers, skeletally thin, a pale-haired man in a long grey coat: Doc Zale.

Dave glanced over his shoulder. They were in a bad place, hemmed in on three sides by the backs of buildings, Jones's photograph gallery, Abby Moorland's millinery and the rear of the *Coffin Creek Epitaph* building.

Jammed together, four men and their horses, in this blind, like cattle in a slaughter pen . . . he glanced at his own horse and saw the rosewood butt of his Winchester carbine jutting from the scabbard on his saddle. There was a carbine on the saddle of Pete's horse too, he remembered.

Joe's thoughts must have been moving along similar lines. He said, 'Get your rifle, Dave. We got range on 'em.'

Dave was thinking about that, watching the three approaching men. There could be no doubt that they were making this way, they even appeared to fan out as they drew nearer, so as to pen the Hooks and McLennans in the backlot . . .

Joe said, 'Dave, get your rifle!'

Dave stepped towards his horse; then he walked past the animal and stood in the open, where the Tengens could see he was unarmed. He could see their faces now, sunspots under their hat brims. Zale, he noticed, was wearing a straw hat. He and Levi each had

148

some kind of weapon cradled across their left forearms; he'd guessed what they were before he heard Joe let out a long breath and declare, 'Jesus! They've got shotguns!'

★ ★ ★

With every ten paces or so, Alva found he had to pause and breathe out slowly; his arms trembled; he was dizzy with fear, or excitement, or anticipation of what he was about to do, or something. He was damp and itchy with sweat, and not just from the sun. He rubbed his damp palms against his black broadcloth jacket and thought, for the thousandth time, about the Smith and Wesson in his pocket. A stranger, walking down the street, came towards him. Alva smiled at the man, showing his teeth, but he guessed his fear showed through the smile, because the stranger gave him a startled, frightened look and hurried past. He could see people were getting off the streets, which had been fairly empty anyway as this was the time of day sensible people took their siesta, but now they hid indoors because they knew what was afoot, the officers of the law were about to take on the outlaw element . . .

Alva smiled at that, a different smile, full of irony. Ahead of them stood the 'outlaw element', the Hooks and the McLennans, the poor damn fools, letting themselves get backed into a corner, hemmed in on three sides.

It was Doc's turn to hold things up now; he paused to do the ritual thing of coughing into his handkerchief, his shoulders shaking. Alva wondered if blood came with his phlegm. Probably. If he was to stop a bullet now, it would be a quick release for him . . . maybe thinking about that was the reason he'd got drunk before doing this thing.

Of the three of them, only Levi seemed calm. Too calm. As if he'd looked into the future and saw it was all black, so all he could do was let the bad cards fall . . .

For a second, Alva felt that too, then he shook the feeling from him. Today, things started going right . . . after today, they'd never look back.

Alva watched the men ahead of him; suddenly he glimpsed the butts of rifles, scabbarded on Pete's horse, on Dave's too. For the first time, another picture came into his mind: he was lying shot in this street, alongside Levi and Doc, and the Hooks and McLennans were walking away, laughing, Pete on his way to see Millie. If they brought those rifles into play, they could cut down their enemies before they got close to shotgun range . . . for a moment, as Dave McLennan walked forward, Alva was certain that was going to happen. Then he saw Dave move away from his horse and stand out in the open . . . that was Dave for you, the law first with him, the legal way first . . . Alva's lips twisted, he could almost feel pity for the man.

Now they were inside shotgun range, forty paces, thirty . . . twenty close enough to see the sweat on the faces of their enemies. The Tengens halted and Zale too. Alva's hands began to shake quite violently, he thrust them into his pockets and gripped the pistol and felt his knuckles whiten; he tried to will the shaking to stop.

Zale, to his right, was staring at him; Levi was further right still. Alva tried to speak and couldn't; his throat was too dry, on fire. When he found the saliva to make words, he said, 'Let them have it.'

Zale cocked one and then the other barrel of the .12 gauge Parker shotgun he held; that was an eloquent enough reply, but he added 'All right' to it. Alva heard Levi also cock his shotgun.

For an instant, the tableau was frozen: four men and their horses, trapped between three walls; three men facing them on the open side. Then Levi called 'You men have made your threats! Go to guns!'

Alva lifted his pistol from his jacket pocket. He glimpsed Levi shifting the shotgun to his left arm, he lifted the Colt in his right hand. Alva touched the deputy sheriff's badge pinned to the pocket of his vest, reminding himself this was going to be legal. Suddenly he was calm, gripped by something like a cold rage. His wrists had ceased their trembling. He lifted his handgun, cocked it and pointed it.

Loud enough for everyone to hear, Levi shouted, 'You know the rules — no guns in town! Hand over your weapons, or go to shooting!'

Dave grabbed the wings of his canvas jacket, pulled them back, showing his shirtfront. He shouted, 'I'm not armed! I've got nothing!'

Billy Hook stepped forward. He said, 'Don't shoot, we don't want any fight!'

Levi called, 'Throw up your hands!'

Dave and Billy lifted their hands above their shoulders, then Pete.

Dave called, 'Levi — '

Alva fired; he shot at Dave but missed. Levi's pistol sounded at almost the same instant, and Zale let go one barrel of the shotgun. Billy fell, as if poleaxed; Dave ducked behind his horse. As Joe sprang forward, he cried, 'I'm not armed!' Zale swung towards him and let go the other barrel of the Parker. Joe went down sprawling and Alva thought Doc had nailed him, but the man scrambled up and ran for it. Alva shot at him, missing again. Joe ducked around the corner of the photograph gallery.

The sudden racket of guns left Alva deafened, he was only now conscious of the screaming of plunging horses, three of which broke clear and bolted down the street. Dave kept a hold of his horse, using the pitching animal as a shield. He seemed to be trying to get his arm over the saddle, reaching for the scabbarded rifle on the far side. The air was dark with powdersmoke, a sickening stench in the nostrils.

Pete stood in the middle of all this, as if rooted. He called something like, 'We don't want to fight!' Alva fired and saw Pete spun half about, his right arm hanging bloodily. Alva fired again, simultaneously with Levi. Pete went down, rolled, drawing his belt gun with his left hand. He fired from the ground. Alva fired at him and hit; he saw the dust jump from the man's shirt, but Pete kept firing.

A bullet must have creased Dave's horse. The animal reared and broke free, running north up the street, leaving Dave in the open. Zale had pushed two more cartridges into the tubes of the Parker, and levelled the shotgun on Dave. Dave called, 'No!' He held out one hand, as if his fingers could turn the power of the weapon.

Zale fired both barrels. Dave was picked up and flung backwards. He screamed as his body struck against the wall; he bounced forward and fell sideways, then lay, kicking. The charge of No. 2 gooseshot had shredded his stomach and abdomen; rags of intestine had come out with the lower wound; there was blood everywhere.

In a high, strangled voice Pete called,

'Dave!' He was still firing. Levi's left leg was knocked from under him and he went down heavily.

Alva gazed at his wounded brother calmly. Pete, hit a half-dozen times, was still moving, trying to thumb cartridges into his emptied pistol. Alva got some cartridges too, but didn't hurry; mechanically he fed them into the chamber of his pistol. Five bullets loaded, he walked over to Pete and lifted his gun and shot him through the chest, then the left shoulder; the gun misfired; he shot Pete through the chest again; there was another misfire and the pistol was empty; but Pete was still alive, writhing against the earth. It didn't seem possible, but there it was.

Doc said, 'Alva. Alva.'

Alva reloaded his pistol. He was raising the weapon when Doc's voice, repeating his name, got through to him. He lowered the gun and stared at Pete. After a time, he became aware of his wider surroundings: Levi sitting up, his bloody leg stretched out before him; Dave McLennan and Billy Hook, lying still; crowds of people forming up on the streets, knots of them drifting towards him. He wanted to vomit; it was the stench of gunpowder did that, he guessed. He asked, 'How is it, Levi?'

His brother gasped in pain. 'Got me through the calf muscle.'

Alva asked, 'Doc?'

'I'm all right. How about you?'

'Not a scratch.'

'Well, we got these sons.'

Alva suddenly remembered something. He walked over to Billy, crouched down by him. He didn't look into the boy's face but took a Colt pistol from his pocket and slid it under the body.

Zale had already dropped a pistol into the dust by Dave McLennan's outstretched right hand. Alva glanced up, to see if anyone was close enough to see him, but the crowds were still only halfway along the street. He stood and tried to compose his face so that no guilt showed.

When the onlookers reached him, three of them lifted Pete McLennan and carried him across the street. Pete was fighting for breath, making whimpering noises. Suddenly, he called out, 'Boys, they have murdered me!'

Alva saw a block of townsfolk coming towards them, not just onlookers, but what looked like a delegation of the town's more respectable citizens. He glanced at Levi, whose face was grey with the shock of his wound. Levi said, 'Well, Alva. We got what you wanted.'

Alva swallowed. 'Almost. Joe got away.'

'Still, it's finished.'

Alva studied the faces of the oncoming delegation. Some showed only fear and shock, others were grave, a few angry, already beginning to judge the Tengens for what they'd done. Alva said, 'Maybe.'

14

Ash Wilson gazed a minute out of the entrance of the adobe, then pushed the steerhide door in place. He said, 'Looks like rain coming. Ain't that a wonderment.'

Taylor had been tugging on his chains whilst his guard's back was turned. Now he sat back against the wall. He was bathed in sweat, and felt dizzy and nauseous. At least his head didn't hurt as badly now. Waves of pain, blinding, white, numbing, only came a couple of times an hour instead of every other minute, as before. As he'd just been suffering from his head wound, he hoped he was due twenty minutes or so respite. He guessed his skull wasn't fractured after all. Taylor wondered if he had enough strength to do what he needed to do next; chained up for two days in this oven of an adobe, with only the bare minimum of food and water, had left him drained, dehydrated and weak.

There was a tin plate of food — beans and a sliver of stringy bacon — on the earth at his feet. He'd been about to eat the food Wilson had offered when his head wound had started aching. Wilson had left it there, while the spell passed. Now Taylor said, 'Pass me the plate, Ash.'

Wilson turned towards him, yawned. He'd left his rifle outside; the grip of a Colt pistol which he wore in a backwards holster high on his right hip, rode up against his bulging stomach. Wilson was slow and dulled with boredom, Taylor supposed, after standing guard for two days. It might be late afternoon, as far as Taylor could judge. There was a damp, fresh feel to the air, the first hint of the rain Wilson had spoken of.

Wilson was obviously in no hurry to feed the prisoner. First, he finished his cigarette, then stamped it underfoot.

He looked out through the doorway again. That suited Taylor; he spent the time testing his chains. The left chain was still unyielding. The right-hand chain was different, the brickwork where the end of the chain was fastened was soft, and he'd been working on it. With a pull of enough strength, he might be able to yank the fixing from the wall . . .

Wilson came over. He looked troubled, Taylor thought. Wilson had his hand on the grip of his pistol. Maybe, Taylor thought, this was the condemned man's last meal. Maybe the business he'd been kept out of was finished, after he'd eaten it would be his turn . . .

Wilson stooped down, wheezing a little as he picked up the plate. He said, 'Don't let no one say we didn't feed you, Taylor.'

Taylor gripped his right wrist with his left hand, jerked his right arm forward. The right-side chain tore loose from the wall in a burst of white dust and flaking brickwork. Wilson started to duck back but Taylor swung the chain. It slapped Wilson alongside the jaw and the side of the head. He grunted and fell to one knee. Taylor hit him in the throat with his elbow and Wilson fell sideways, hands cupped under his chin, choking.

Taylor grabbed Wilson's pistol and pulled the gun out from under the man's weight. Wilson broke free, rolled away from Taylor and got to his feet, lunging for the doorway. He was almost there when Taylor fired. The shot struck the wall by the door jamb, drove a spume of dust and plaster back into Wilson's face. He staggered backwards, coughing, his hands raised. Taylor cocked the pistol again.

Wilson cried, 'Don't shoot! Oh God! Don't shoot!'

'Then get back over here! Over here, you bag of guts! Get down on your face, here!'

The reinsman obeyed, lowering his bulk to the floor. Taylor jammed the muzzle of the pistol into Wilson's left temple. The reinsman's left eye edged sideways and fixed on the front sight of the gun.

Taylor said, 'Keys! Get the keys!'

Wilson seemed to be trying to bury his face in the earth, at the same time his left eye stared in fascination at the pistol barrel. He said, 'Oh God! Oh God! Don't shoot! Don't shoot, Taylor! I didn't kill your friends!'

Taylor gasped as a new wave of pain crashed through his head. He thought, don't let me pass out before I get free. He hung his head a moment, breathing slowly and the dizziness subsided. Wilson looked like he might be praying soundlessly, or was about to start weeping, or both. He closed his eyes tightly, waiting for the bullet.

Taylor asked, 'What friends?'

15

Joe Hook sat in the main funeral parlour in Coffin Creek. He stared at the floor turning his hat brim between his fingers to give his hands something to do. Outside, the night was black with rain, arabesques of rain striped the windows, coursing downwards, the rushing of water filling Joe's ears. 'It's a real gully-washer,' Joe said, to nobody in particular.

The only person who could have heard him was the undertaker, standing a few paces away, a spare, grey-haired man in black, his thin face bearing a suitable expression of gravitas. He asked, 'Is everything as you would wish it, Mr Hook?'

Joe nodded.

'I'll leave you then.'

Joe nodded again, glancing at the undertaker as the man turned to leave. He kept his features composed in solemn dignity but Joe could see something else behind his eyes: boredom. This was a scene he played out every day of the week, a ritual path he had followed a thousand times. And maybe there was something else, something behind the boredom, something personal, specific to Joe: contempt.

The undertaker left. Now there were four men in the room, but the others couldn't see Joe; their eyes were closed, their faces towards the window, the glass with slivers of rain streaking down it, the wild night outside; deaf to the sound of the storm. To anything. The undertaker had composed their faces as best he could: Billy looked like he was in a light sleep, Pete appeared to be smiling slightly, a look of vague irritation lay on Dave's face. A wonder how the undertaker had managed that; Joe had seen Dave after the shooting, his mouth wide in a cry of pain, his face twisted in his final agony. It would have been better, Joe thought, to have left Dave that way, so that his face mirrored the ugly reality of his final seconds. Dave, Pete, Billy, none of them had deserved to die; only he'd deserved a bullet, and the other men who'd walked away from the fight . . . They should have left Dave the way he'd died, his expression saying, Boys, they have murdered me! just as Pete had said it.

The dead men faced the rain, deaf to the noise Joe was making, strangled, grunting noises, like a man trying to hold back tears, or a frustrated scream of rage. His fingers closed about the brim of the hat, stretching and bending the material; he began to tear at the hat and then he got hold of himself. Maybe it was the look behind the undertaker's eyes that had got to him, what he thought he'd seen there . . . the contempt.

Joe told the room, 'I'm not a coward!'

So he'd run, he'd run and let his

brother die, and the McLennans. What else could he have done: *he was unarmed*? What else could he have done, taken on the Tengens with his bare hands, faced Zale's shotgun like that? He said, 'I'm not a coward!'

The dead men weren't listening. They lay in their broadcloth suits, hands folded neatly on their chests, covering the ruin underneath, the carnage left by guns. Three dead men in their coffins, gazing out into the crashing darkness, seeing and hearing none of it. Did they see or hear anything else, now? Joe didn't believe they did. Each of these men had only their three score years and ten, and the Tengens had stolen half of Dave's time, and two-thirds of Billy and Pete's time. Jesus, Billy was only nineteen! At least he hadn't known much about what had been done to him, nor had Dave; but Pete had died hard, as bravely as anyone Joe had ever seen. Maybe there was an afterlife, after all, and right now Billy was saying to Pa, 'If you'd been more like me, Pa, you wouldn't have got killed!' And Pa would sneer out of the grey tangle of his beard and say, 'Oh yes? Then why're you here, and not your brother Joe?'

The rain slackened briefly. Through the black windows Joe saw the yellow, blurred lights of the town behind the downpour. Off at the other end of town, the Tengens and their gang would be celebrating . . . no murder charges brought against them, the town seemed to have swallowed the Tengens and *the Epitaph's* version of events, that the dead men had been armed and dangerous, that the Tengens had been forced to fire on them when they refused to hand over their guns . . . it looked like the Tengens were going to get away with it and Alva'd have the election in the bag.

Tomorrow, when the rain cleared, people on the streets outside would be able to stare through the windows into the peaceful faces of these dead men, faces that ought to be contorted in pain and anger, shouting, *Boys, they have murdered me!* For a moment, Joe wondered if he ought to have the coffins moved, so that the corpses weren't on display so openly . . . but no. Let this town look on its own guilt and shame. Look on and think. Maybe even the Tengens might look into the faces of these men and think, too, if they had any conscience left at all.

A third time Joe told the dead men, 'I'm not a coward.' But they couldn't hear. There was only one way for him to prove his courage. He glanced up the rain-lashed street, at the dim, wavering lights of the buildings seeing, in his mind's eye, the inside of the Long Branch, hearing the noise and the hard laughter of men. He remembered there was a .12 gauge Parker shotgun in the saddle pack on his horse . . . ironic that, a Parker, the very weapon the Tengens and Zale had used on Dave and on Billy . . .

★ ★ ★

169

Alva said, 'Black in the top pocket.'

He leaned on his cue a moment, took his time with the shot, potted the black. 'Game,' he declared, and smirked foolishly.

The pool and billiards room at the back of the Long Branch was crowded tonight, and all of them friends of the Tengens and Zale, except Zale wasn't here; for the first time Levi could remember Doc had let his sickness drive him to bed. But there were plenty of men to buy Levi a drink, slap his back, pump his hand, congratulate him and ask questions too stupid to answer.

Alva was on a winning streak on the pool table; he always claimed he played better when he was drunk. It was rare to see Alva drunk at all, he was normally careful of himself, but not tonight . . .

Levi's head ached, even though he hadn't drunk much tonight, even at this celebration. He still felt feverish from his leg wound, although it wasn't much at all; the bullet had gone straight through, he could still stand on it. Suddenly he'd had enough of the smoke and the noise and the meaningless questions. He told Alva, 'I'm going home.'

Alva looked faintly outraged a moment, then he said, 'Let the boys go with you!'

The 'boys' stepped forward. Turkey Creek Jack Green and Sherman Andersson.

Levi said, 'No, thanks.'

Turkey Creek said, 'Ain't safe, Levi. Not with Joe Hook still out on the streets.'

Levi said, 'The day I'm scared of trash like him, I'll quit this business.'

Alva glared. Levi discovered something about himself, something he didn't like. He was scared of Alva drunk. He didn't know why that was, maybe the craziness in Alva, that he normally kept in check, showed when he was the worse for drink . . . then, he didn't know what the man would do.

Maybe it was something others saw in Alva that made them wary of him, for all his attempts to be all things to all men. Levi knew Alva's schemes would all come to ruin, he'd lead Levi into disaster, and anyone else who followed him . . . but he was Levi's brother, after all . . .

Alva said, 'Go with him, boys.'

Now it was Levi's turn to glare. He said, 'I said no, Alva.'

It was a tone of voice he hadn't used on Alva in, he didn't know how long; perhaps not since he'd first been a man, and Alva was still the kid brother, still a boy, and they'd both known it. Alva looked at him owlishly. For a second he looked like that boy he'd been then. He said, 'But Levi — '

Levi took his hat. 'I'll be all right.'

Alva stared, a little too long. He nodded slowly, 'All right, Levi.'

Levi said, 'I'll be all right,' again, this time to Turkey Creek and Andersson. They glared at him doubtfully. He turned towards the door, wincing with sudden pain as he began to drag his injured leg. A man came in through the door. He was soaked through. He shook his hands of rain and declared, 'It's a real gully-washer out there!'

Levi pulled on his 'fish', the yellow oilskin slicker with the fish brand mark on it and stepped out into the rain. It drove into his face, obliterating visibility; even the brooding shape of Apache Peak, overlooking the town, was lost behind the grey screen of rain. Now Cochise County was cold and wet as anywhere; tomorrow it would be once again, the desert, the mountains, hot enough to strip paint and dry as the inside of a furnace.

Levi took the most direct route home, down main street, then turned left, near to where the AT corral sign hung creaking under the downpour. Maybe, he thought, he didn't have to follow Alva's scheme all the way; maybe better now to cut and run. That was what his wife wanted; she'd been urging him for weeks to take them somewhere else, away from here ... but there had been Alva, with his big plans, schemes that, for once, wouldn't go wrong.

He said, 'Damn you Alva.' But it wasn't right just to blame his brother; maybe part of him was as wild, for all he was a married, settled man. After all he'd gone along with this so far ... and Alva *was* right, if it did work out, the prize was a whole county, the whole south-east corner of Arizona would be theirs, to plunder at will.

He made slow going, limping through the mud. The unexpected pain of his wound brought a little sweat to his face. He swore at the rain which had already soaked him through, despite his slicker. He squinted through the greyness ahead of him, at the empty street. And then a man stepped from the shadows and came towards him.

The downpour thinned a little; Levi felt the beat of it slacken on the brim of his hat. The approaching man drew closer. Levi wasn't surprised to see it was Joe Hook; he realized he'd been expecting him.

Joe wore a long slicker, the rain had crumpled his hat over his head and he held what looked like a Parker shotgun in his right hand, barrel pointing at the earth. Behind Joe, moonlight flashed on the puddles that pitted the street.

Lifting his voice over the hissing rain, Levi said, 'Joe.' He glanced at the shotgun; it was a Parker all right. He ought to be frightened of so terrible a weapon but strangely enough, he wasn't. He felt curiously calm, at ease.

Joe said, 'I wanted Alva. Or Zale.'

'You've got me.'

'I wanted Alva.'

You're not going to get him, Levi decided. He brushed aside the folds of his slicker, so he could reach the grip of his right-hand Colt. He thought, what if the cartridges are damp, and misfire? For the first time, fear touched him, but it wasn't for himself, it was for Alva. Levi balanced himself on his feet, the wound in his calf sending a sharp pain lancing through him, but it was nothing really; he was steady enough and he could get his belt gun into action before this clod could use the scattergun. He said, 'You son-of-a-bitching cowboy, get your gun and get to work!'

Joe stared.

Levi felt his lips twist into a sneer. He said, 'You yellow bastard!'

Joe made a choked sound. He started to raise the shotgun and Levi pulled his beltgun. He took his time, centred on Joe's chest, fired. And heard the sound of a misfire! The twin mouths of the shotgun were gaping at him, he half-turned left; then a terrible impact struck his left arm. He was smashed from his feet, flung headlong, ploughing into the mud on his face. His hat was gone, rain coursed down his face. He felt pain then, more pain than he'd ever known, and screamed. He screamed into the sound of the shotgun, which still echoed around him, thunder in his ears. He saw his Colt lying in the mud a yard before his face. With his right hand, he reached towards it. He watched the rain stipple the earth before him. Behind him he heard Joe cock the second barrel of the Parker. As Levi got his hand to the pistol he was thinking, Joe'll let me have it in the back of the skull, he'll blow my head off, that's where I'd put it, if I was avenging my brother. He waited for the impact. But when it came it smashed against the lower left side, slamming him face down, driving him into the mud ... A long time after that he heard voices, men shouting, and running feet, splashing through the mud, coming towards him ... but he felt no pain, even when hands lifted him and he was being carried ...

Dimly, he became aware of his surroundings: he was back in the Long Branch, they'd stretched him out over the pool table! The green baize was darker now, blood glued him to it. Faces swam about him, turning into kerosene lamps and lights and back to faces again.

Alva's face was there, twisted, bloodless, red-striped with tears. Alva was crying, 'Levi!' again and again.

Someone was mopping the rain off his face with a handkerchief, brushing back the damp hair plastered to his forehead.

A voice asked, 'Who was it, Levi?'

Levi tried to lift his head, but blood, a huge, sticky lake of it, was sucking him down, anchoring him to the table. Finally, he managed to say, 'It was Joe. Joe Hook.'

He heard a voice call, 'Where's the doctor?' A waste of time, he thought, when it came to shotguns, except if you got the victims to a hospital, only there was no hospital in Coffin Creek, nothing nearer than Tucson, and that was seventy-five miles . . . someone called 'Get his wife!' Levi smiled at that, that made more sense . . .

But he didn't see his wife. The last face he remembered seeing was Alva's, a deathmask without colour, except for the red wounds the tear stripes had gouged in his cheeks, below his crazed eyes . . . that was fitting, Levi thought, because this business was all about brothers, and the ties that bound them. He was trying to speak to Alva, to the ghostly face that hung above him. At last he heard himself say, 'It won't be long. Are my legs stretched out straight and my boots off?'

Alva nodded very slowly. He said, 'Levi, Levi!'

Levi smiled.

16

Zale said, 'Alva, listen to me.'

He didn't think Alva was listening to anything. They both sat at the table in the back room of the Long Branch, but Alva had twisted around, sitting with his back to the table, staring at the floor. He rested his head in his hands.

Zale could hear the dim buzz of voices in the saloon; they could only be talking about one thing. Levi's wife had come and they'd taken Levi home. He supposed the swampers were out, cleaning the pool hall, making it look less like a butcher's yard. Levi had bled so much; it was astonishing that anyone had that much blood in him, soaking the pool table through.

Doc drank off his whiskey. The spirit burned inside him, hurt him terribly, but now everything hurt him terribly. He said, 'Alva.'

Alva made a sound, not a word, but a formless noise acknowledging that he'd heard, at least.

'Alva,' Zale said, 'we've got to get Joe.'

'Joe?'

'We've got to get Joe,' Zale repeated, as though explaining to a child. 'Kill him if we can, but get him anyway.'

'Joe.'

'Someone said he was seen hiding out around the McLennan place. That's where we should look. Not around the Hook ranch. Alva, are you listening?'

Alva stretched his long, pale fingers out before him, gazed at them stupidly.

Zale said, 'Tonight, Alva! We need to get going now!'

'Not now.'

Zale felt wild impatience mount in him; that hurt, too, everything he did brought pain. He'd never had much patience to begin with, but these last few years, as his sickness took hold, he'd none left; he flew into the worst rages over nothing.

But he needed to keep his temper now, he realized, if anything was to be salvaged, if everything wasn't going to end in complete ruin. His thin lips twisted with irony at the last thought . . . what was he doing, worrying about the future, when his could be measured in months, not years? But Alva still had a future left in him, providing he did just the right thing now and seeing Alva succeed, get away with it, that would be some compensation for the dirty trick fate had played on Zale, that would be paying the world one dirty trick back . . .

'Alva,' Doc said, with all the patience he could muster, 'we do it tonight. We need to shut Joe up. We'll take him, kill him if we can . . . '

Alva nodded slowly. 'All right.'

'Only, for God's sake, we've got to make it look like he was killed fair.' Zale paused, even a little talking got him breathless now. He produced a handkerchief, began to cough gently into the white lace.

Alva said, 'What about Luke and Ira?'

'God knows where they are. Maybe they got themselves killed somewhere in Mexico. No need to worry about them. Just Joe.'

'Just Joe.' Alva formed his hands into fists. 'You think you've got the world by the tail, all things coming right, and then . . . '

'It can still go right, Alva. Most of this town believes what you told 'em about shooting the McLennans and Billy. You're a hero to them!'

'I am?'

'Sure. And the election next month . . . you've got it in the bag! Especially now, with — '

Alva lifted his head, he stared at the other man. 'With what?'

Zale didn't answer immediately. He poured and drank another whiskey, gasping as the alcohol seared down inside him, as his insides seemed to bunch and tighten about the fierce flame of the liquor. He said, 'With

Levi, and all. Guarantees you the sympathy vote.'

Alva's mouth twisted. He laughed harshly. 'The sympathy vote.'

'But first we need to get Joe.'

'Yes.' Alva got to his feet. The look on his face wasn't pleasant to see; it frightened Zale, the first time he'd been frightened of anything in he didn't know how long.

* * *

They took Joe as he rode out of the McLennan ranch. The rain had eased to a thin spitting drizzle, raising a fine mist, and a blue full moon showed behind dark and swollen clouds. There were four of them: Zale, Alva, Turkey Creek Green, Sherman Andersson. Turkey Creek always fanced himself a handy man with a rope; they waited in some cover until Joe rode by, then Turkey Creek cast his rope and the noose fell over Joe's shoulders, whisking him out of the saddle as easy as you please. Joe landed badly in the mud, which splattered his face and his shirt; Andersson and Green both laughed at that. Green yanked Joe to his feet and covered him with his handgun. Alva and Zale both dismounted and approached their prisoner.

Joe wasn't wearing a belt gun although the butt of a rifle poked from the scabbard on his saddle. Alva got to Joe first. Before Zale could stop him, Alva raised his fist and knocked Joe down. Zale stared; in all the years he'd known Alva, he'd never known him use his hands that way, he was always so careful of them. He glimpsed, in the moonlight, the craziness in Alva's eyes. Alva lifted his Smith and Wesson from his jacket pocket but Zale put one hand on his arm and shouted, 'Alva, wait!'

Alva stared at him, as if he'd never seen the man before. 'Wait for what, Doc?'

Joe got to his feet. The punch had put a flush along his right cheekbone, but the man didn't seem afraid; he smiled at his captors with something like contempt.

Andersson asked, 'Yes, wait for what?'

'If we do it, it's got to look right. We can't mess it up, now. Alva, you listening?'

Nobody said anything for a minute. Joe looked around him, still smiling in disdain, his eyes sullen and unafraid.

Alva breathed out slowly. 'Sure, Doc.'

Zale told Joe, 'Get on your horse.'

Joe asked, 'Why not do it here? You're going to have to shut me up. If I'm going to be killed resisting arrest, why not do it now?'

'What makes you think you're going to get it at all?'

'You got any brothers, Zale?'

Zale blinked, surprised by the question. 'Only child.'

'Then you don't understand.'

'Get on your horse.'

Andersson reached over, lifted the

gun from the scabbard on Joe's saddle.
It was a shotgun. Andersson declared,
'This is a Parker.'

Alva said, 'A Parker.' The word made
a strangled sound in his throat. Zale saw
his face, stiff, composed, barely human,
change; his face contorted with hatred
and pain, it was for an instant the face
of a frightened, angry child, close to
tears. Zale could see Alva was very near
to losing all control. Zale stepped close
to him; he lowered his voice against the
whisper of the rain, so that perhaps only
Alva would hear. He said, urgently,
'Alva, if we do this, it's got to look
right. Remember what's at stake. All
you and Levi worked for.'

After a moment, Alva said, 'All
right.'

'So we don't kill him yet.'

'All right.'

He studied Alva's face in the moonlight, watched the features settle back
into their calm mask. Doc sighed,
surprised at the relief he felt; his head
ached dully. He walked over to Joe.

The man gazed about him, wary as a trapped animal. Zale produced his own pistol, jabbed Joe in the ribs harder than he needed to and said, 'Well, get mounted, goddammit!'

Joe turned, stepped towards his horse, put his hands on the saddle. Zale, standing just behind him, felt the wind of the bullet. Joe was knocked forward against the horse and the animal shied away. It screamed, kicking out both hind legs, and broke forward into the space between Green and Andersson, bolting into the darkness. Joe was face down in the mud; he squirmed over on to his side. The moonlight limned his upturned face, his gaping mouth, the wild look in his eyes.

Zale cried, 'Alva!'

Alva stepped forward, the Smith and Wesson lifted for a second shot. Zale sprang forward, the sudden movement putting fire and pain in his chest. He grabbed Alva's arm. With a sudden, violent movement, Alva threw the arm off and Doc staggered backwards; he fell to one knee, toppled forward and steadied himself with one arm. He had to fight for breath; he began coughing. He heard Alva say, 'You were right, Joe. About brothers.'

Zale lifted his head and saw Alva standing over the fallen man, pistol raised. Joe looked like he was trying to move on to his back, then Alva's gun banged: Joe slammed face down in the mud. Zale called, 'Alva! You'll ruin it! You'll ruin everything!' but the words were lost in the explosion of shots, three more, almost together. Alva used his foot to turn Joe over, so he lay face up to the moonlight, arms flung wide. Zale heard his rasping, tortured breathing and saw the man try to lift his head; five shots in the back and he was still alive! Alva was carefully and unhurriedly thumbing shells into his pistol, smiling a very little, his face showing nothing otherwise. He lifted the pistol and fired five times into Joe's face, so that when the gun was emptied there was nothing left, nothing to recognize, no human features, only a sodden pulp of blood and bone matter, caved in on itself like a rotten fruit.

Zale sucked helplessly for breath. When he found some, he said, 'Well, you done it, Alva! That's torn it now!'

17

A procession wound into Coffin Creek from the south, from the Mexican quarter. Three light wagons, each pulled by a single dark horse. The horses moved at a bare walk. Figures between the vehicles moved slowly too. They were all dressed in sombre clothing, eyes fixed on the earth. A small Indian boy led the column, banging a slow beat on a hoop drum; he was followed by an old Indian astride a ribshot pony — it looked like the old man had fallen asleep in the saddle. A full warbonnet of ragged feathers drooped over his head, stirred by the wind that sifted a thin, gauzy dust across the street. The rain had passed, the land was again bone dry, hot and sunbleached.

Calvin Taylor stood on the sidewalk, a little apart from the sizeable crowd of onlookers and studied the two Indians.

191

Probably locals, Pimas or Papagos, although the oldster was got up like a Sioux or Cheyenne chief. Arizona Indians didn't go in for feathers and warbonnets like Plains Indians, and the townsfolk must have known it, but maybe the undertaker felt the need to add a picturesque touch to things. Similarly, there were long black plumes fastened to the collars of the horses that drew each wagon. Taylor glimpsed the polished, silver-chased coffins in each vehicle. Ahead of the first hearse walked a young man in black and an old woman holding a parasol aloft whose face was masked by a grey veil. Taylor supposed this was Joe Hook's mother and his remaining brother. Further back in the column were some other women in mourning clothes. All the dead men were bachelors, but they'd have had sweethearts, maybe even Dave. Was Millie Tengen part of the slow, grim line? Taylor ought to be there, too, for Dave's sake, but he hated funerals; Dave would understand him not being part of it. Half of the town seemed to have turned out, to pay their respects and the last two men in the column held a long banner between them. It had black lettering on a white background, the legend reading: WILLIAM HOOK, DAVID McLENNAN, PETER McLENNAN and, underneath, MURDERED IN THE STREETS OF COFFIN CREEK.

Schneider came and stood alongside Taylor. They watched the procession turn off the main thoroughfare and climb the road to the cemetery. The kid kept the same dull, slow beat on the hollow drum, a sound like a tap dripping that worked at Taylor's nerves. His head wound ached. He squinted into the waves of heat that rippled over the desert floor.

Schneider still looked as if a herd of buffalo had passed over him. Blue-black bruises looped around his eyes, which had yellow discolorations below them; his lower lip was still swollen.

Taylor said, 'It doesn't seem to have worked.'

'Uh?'

'The Tengens plan to frame these men . . . the town doesn't seem to have bought it, after all.'

'The *Epitaph* is still trying to defend them. But there were too many witnesses who swore Dave and Billy were unarmed, too many who saw the killings . . . '

' 'The gunfight at the AT corral' you mean? That's what the *Epitaph* called it.'

Schneider put a hand in his mouth, perhaps feeling for a loosened tooth. 'Except it wasn't a gunfight, and it happened behind Abby Moorland's millinery store.'

' 'Gunfight at the AT corral' has got more of a ring to it than 'The killing at Abby Moorland's millinery'. You all right?'

Schneider took his hand from his mouth. 'I'm all right. I sure wasn't letting those sons of bitches run me out of town. I feel like hell, but I'm still topside. Walking around alive's getting to be a rarity around here. There's those out there' — Schneider nodded after the funeral procession, — 'and in a few days they'll have to come back and plant Joe.'

'Joe was the only one who deserved killing. Him and Levi.'

Schneider smiled ironically. 'That's for God to decide, isn't it?'

'That sounds like something Dave McLennan would have said. He was always keen on sticking to the letter of the law.' Taylor added bitterly, 'Look what it got him.'

After a little pause, Schneider said, 'The Tengens did have it sewed up, at one point. If they hadn't killed Joe that way . . . Now Alva and Zale are wanted for murder. The president himself — he's threatened to put this whole county under martial law if it doesn't put its house in order. So much for the Tengens, the law-bringers!'

Taylor nodded. 'Now they're my business, too.'

'How so?'

'Ash Wilson's singing like a bird. Seems the Tengens were tied in with Joe over half the stage hold-ups down here. Wells Fargo business, so that makes it my business.'

'So you're going after them?'

Taylor grunted a yes.

Schneider asked, 'You know where to look? Mexico? Up in the hills?'

'Alva's a town boy. He ain't gonna stay out in the wild country long. And Zale's too sick to travel rough. I've a hunch where they're running for.'

'And where's that?'

'I heard of one bad egg, wanted in Arizona, he got to Colorado and found he couldn't be extradited. So Alva might go there.'

Schneider gazed off to the north-east, at blue mountains running against the sky. 'There's a lot of mean country between here and Colorado.'

Taylor nodded. 'And that's where I'll find Alva Tengen.'

18

Late in the afternoon of the next day, Calvin Taylor rode into a clearing; it was an opening in a good stand of timber. He was up in high mountain country now, far above the desert, a different world; a green and blue world of pine forests under mountains streaked with snow, where there were occasional lakes and streams of rushing water. This was the best country in the south-west, with water, timber and game. The Apaches had seized it, made their strongholds here whilst they raided the lower country. Taylor decided that was something to think about, with the reservation not too far north.

He was north-east of the Dragoons, climbing into the Peloncillos, tomorrow he'd cross into New Mexico. Earlier today, he'd met a Mexican sheepherder who'd seen a party of Anglos passing at a distance heading north-east. Four men; one of them seemed sick, he rode slumped in the saddle. Alva, Turkey Creek, Sherman Andersson, Zale. It was Zale who was holding them up. Travelling this kind of country, breathing the thin air, must be killing him by inches. If they'd cut loose of Zale, the others could be halfway to Colorado now.

Taylor was riding a roan gelding and everything he needed was in the saddle-roll behind him. Travelling so light, he expected to come up with his quarry early tomorrow.

He was wrong by twelve hours: he met them five minutes later, about 400 yards east of the clearing.

Taylor had got careless; part of him was admiring the country, the wild beauty of the landscape, instead of scanning it for enemies. Whilst he was sight-seeing a noosed rope fell over his shoulders. Before he could free himself the rope was pulled tight, pinning his arms to his sides and he was jerked backwards. He landed on his rump, impact jolting the teeth in his head; for a minute he was both sick and dizzy with shock. In that time, four riders came from the trees, two behind him, two ahead.

Slowly, Taylor got to his feet. One rider ahead of him had caught the roan by the reins, held the animal; that was Alva Tengen. Zale was behind him.

He turned and studied the other two men: Sherman Andersson and Turkey Jack Green. The latter held the rope. Taylor lifted the noose and slipped it over his head. Green said, 'Get rid of your gun.' He held a pistol in his hand, Alva also. Taylor removed his gunbelt, dropped it to the grass. Alva slid the Winchester out of the saddle on Taylor's horse.

Alva dismounted and walked towards Taylor, then Andersson. The latter got to him first. Taylor was watching Alva and he wasn't ready for the punch Andersson swung. It caught him on the jaw and knocked him sprawling. Taylor shook his head, sick and dizzy again; he heard Andersson and Green laughing. He knew the kind of men they were; the men who did Alva's dirty work for him, like beating up Schneider, men with a taste for violence.

Alva said, 'Glad you could join us, Taylor. We was just about to make camp.'

Zale coughed and said, 'Kill the son of a bitch now, Alva. Why wait?'

Taylor felt a little shocked, looking at Zale. His greyness was now white as ashes; he looked like a ghost, a man who ought not to be alive. When he started coughing into his handkerchief again, his thin shoulders heaved violently. Zale lifted his head and Taylor glimpsed blood on his lips. He made the usual noises, fighting for breath.

Alva said, 'You forget, Henry. I still plan to beat this murder charge. Once we get to Colorado, I can sit it out, wait till things quiet down. So I don't want to leave any more corpses along my trail.'

Green was coiling his rope. 'What then?'

'Tomorrow, about mid-morning, we go past this place. A canyon about six feet across and a mile deep. The perfect place to drop off a body, where it won't ever be found. And if it is . . . '

Andersson rubbed his grazed knuckles. He grinned. 'And if it is . . . ?'

'We can make it look like Apaches done it. Shoot him in the head, then chop his head off. I heard the Apaches do that sometimes, behead their victims.'

Taylor tried to stand, the world rocked about him, he sat back. Andersson had something of a punch on him, he decided.

Green asked, 'Why'd the Apaches do that?'

Alva smiled a very little. 'Ask Taylor.'

Taylor said, 'A trick they learned

from the Yaquis.' Again, he tried to stand; this time he succeeded.

Alva said, 'Well, you learn something every day. I'd heard you were an Indian expert.'

Green laughed. 'Expert on their women, I hear. That true Taylor? You prefer red bitches to white women?'

Andersson said, 'A white woman ain't gonna touch a man who's been with squaws — squaws is all he can get!' He and Green laughed.

Alva glanced at them, a little distaste showing in his eyes. He said, 'We'll camp in that clearing back there. Hold out your hands, Taylor.'

Taylor thrust both his hands before him. Alva stepped forward and clamped handcuffs around Taylor's wrists. The grip was tight, an angle of metal bit into the underside of his right wrist. Despite himself, he winced with pain. Alva smiled very faintly. He said, 'Don't worry. You won't be wearing 'em after tomorrow morning.'

They made a fire of deadwood, eating

a frugal evening meal; Taylor was fed, too. Afterwards, Green and Andersson got into a conversation punctuated by loud laughter. Doc drank whiskey and coughed. Neither Alva nor Taylor talked for a while, then Alva said, 'Doc, next settlement we come to, we'll leave you there.'

'Like hell!'

'You can lie low.'

'I can lie low in Colorado. I can't be extradited there.'

Alva poured coffee into his tin cup. 'Henry, you won't make it to Colorado.'

'I'll be there ahead of you, you sonofabitch!' He laughed harshly, which turned into another coughing fit.

Alva laughed also, a sudden, jarring sound. Alva looked to be in a good humour, something that puzzled Taylor. He gazed at the prisoner. 'You disappoint me, Taylor.'

'I do?'

'Aren't you curious about this business? About how things happened?'

'I know most of it. You wanted to shut up all the witnesses to the stage hold-up. What I don't understand is why you turned against Joe.'

Alva stared into his coffee a moment. 'I had a plan. I wanted to shut up two of the boys in the hold-up: but Joe wouldn't go along with it. That's what started it all.'

'What boys? Ira and Luke?'

Alva blinked. 'You know about them?'

Taylor laughed.

Sherman Andersson asked, 'What's so goddam funny?'

Taylor laughed again. 'You wanted to shut up Ira and Luke? No need.'

Alva threw the grounds of his coffee into the fire. 'What do you mean?'

'I trailed Ira and Luke into Mexico. I took care of them.'

Green was picking his teeth with what looked like a long piece of wire. He asked, 'You killed them?'

'I killed Luke. The boy, Ira, he shot himself rather than be took.'

Green took the wire from his mouth. 'Jesus!'

'They been dead since the day after the hold-up.'

Alva got to his feet and stepped away from the fire. He stood in silence a minute, the knuckles of one hand pressed to his lips. Then he asked Taylor, 'Did either of 'em talk first?'

'No. Ira shot himself rather than talk.'

'So why didn't you say anything?'

'At first . . . I dunno. Then I thought if I kept quiet about it, it might put a tangle in your plans.'

As if talking to himself, Alva said, 'Since the day after the hold-up. Dead since then. So all this . . . we didn't need to do any of it. Killing the McLennans, what happened to Joe . . . and Levi . . . '

A look of pain crossed Alva's face, Taylor might almost have felt sorry for him, but for his mentioning of the McLennans. Taylor said, 'It would have happened anyway. Sooner or later, you'd've turned against your friends. You know why?'

That little tic was pulsing in Alva's cheek again, Taylor saw. The man had composed his face, he seemed calm, but that tiny mannerism gave away what he was really feeling; he was stretched tight as a bow-string, ready to let his violence explode. He asked, 'Why?'

' 'Cos you're a mad dog, Alva.'

Alva's lips twisted with contempt, as if he'd been hoping for a better insult. 'You think so?'

Taylor opened his mouth to reply and Alva kicked him in the chest. Taylor went back, sprawling, gasping for breath. Alva walked around the fire, came towards him.

Green slipped the tooth-picking wire back into the top pocket of his fringed jacket. 'We could kill this feller now, and pack the body up to the canyon. We don't need him alive any more.'

Andersson said, 'Let's kill him now, Alva!'

'No.'

'Why wait?'

Alva returned to the fire, sat down. Taylor got to his knees, began to rub his chest.

Alva poured himself some more coffee. 'I can still win in this business. Soon as the ruckus in Coffin Creek settles down, I can get back on track. I can get what I want.'

'What's that?' Taylor asked, a little hoarsely. 'Build up the legend of Alva Tengen?'

Tengen's eyes got a slightly wild gleam in them. He chuckled. 'That's right. Who knows? In fifty years' time they might be saying I was the greatest lawman there ever was. The man who tamed the West!'

'Sure.'

Alva fished in one pocket of his jacket and produced the deputy marshal's badge. 'Funny how I can't let go of this thing.' He held the star by one point and turned it, so that firelight gleamed redly on the dull tin. 'How much do you weigh?' He looked at Taylor. 'You'd be surprised what people will believe. I guess they believe what they want to believe, so you tell them the stories they want to hear. I'll be a big name when you're just a pile of bones at the bottom of a canyon. So you wanted to tangle up my plans . . . '

'It worked, didn't it?'

Andersson made an impatient sound. 'Goddam it, Alva! 'Cos of him, this whole business went bad. Kill him now!'

Alva slipped the badge back into his pocket. 'Tomorrow. Let him sweat a little. You got about twelve hours, Taylor. Think about that.'

Andersson said, 'It's 'cos of him Levi got killed! Your brother!'

'That's something,' Alva said, 'I'll be thinking about.'

19

Next morning, at breakfast, Alva seemed once again in excellent spirits. He told the prisoner, 'By dark, we ought to be out of this stinking Arizona. New territory. I can start over.'

Taylor clenched and unclenched his hands, wondering how strong they were after half a day in the tight clasp of the cuffs. He asked, 'How's your legend this morning?'

Alva smiled, showing his teeth. 'It's amazing what you can get people to believe. I gave it 'em all . . . how I hunted buffalo, cleaned up the Kansas cow-towns, faced down all the bad men you ever heard of. Bullshit, all of it . . . but the wilder the story, the more they believed it. Well, let's pull out.' He got to his feet. 'You know, Taylor, I'll be almost sorry to pull the trigger on you.' He glanced at Green and Andersson; they had their backs to him and contempt showed openly in his face. 'It's good to have an intelligent conversation.'

'You could always change your mind.'

Alva's eyes grew chilly, the humour disappeared from his face. 'Not a chance.'

As Alva turned away, Taylor thought, *You're wrong. There's one chance — in the pocket of Turkey Creek Jack Green's jacket.*

Zale had spent the last hour or so coughing. He had to be lifted into the saddle, where he slumped against the neck of his horse. His face was bloodless, twisted in pain and exhaustion. They rode out of camp, heading north-east. Alva took the lead, he led Zale's horse whilst Doc hung in the saddle. Next came Green, then the prisoner, with Andersson bringing up the rear.

The trail began to climb steeply, thinning to little more than a goat track. It threaded between ranks of spruce, Douglas fir and ponderosa pine. Wild, empty country, unspoiled by the rock-scratchers or those who followed them. They climbed to a ridge, a spine rising above the surrounding terrain. Timber thinned around them, snow-capped mountains wheeled on either side. It was sometimes hot, the high sun burning fiercely, and then cold, as a gusty wind tugged at them, a sharp cold wind off the mountain peaks.

Taylor had no time to appreciate magnificent scenery, his mind was on other things. Such as how the trail narrowed until it was only a few paces wide, so that the riders had to move along it single-file, with dizzy straight-down drops in places along the way. Now the trail started to switch about, so that he began to lose sight of the riders ahead of him, and Andersson behind.

If he was going to try anything, Taylor decided, now was the time. His captors were strung out along the ridge, out of sight of each other in places. But what could he do, handcuffed as he was? Even if he ran for it, jumped out of the saddle and slithered downslope into the timber, how far could he get without a gun?

Green, ahead of him, turned his horse suddenly. He rode back to Taylor, who reined in his own horse.

Green said, 'You ain't tied enough for me.' He had to raise his voice above the wind. He lifted a Colt pistol from his jacket pocket and trained it on the prisoner's chest. 'Grab hold of your saddle horn.'

Taylor did as instructed. From somewhere, Green produced about three yards of rope. He transferred his Colt to his left hand and leaned forward with the rope in his right hand.

If he was going to tie the captive's wrists to the saddle horn, Taylor guessed, he'd have to take his hands off the pistol at least once. Taylor calculated that Sherman Andersson, out of sight behind a screen of stooped, wind-thrashed trees, would come into view in about one minute. Alva and Zale had got about the same distance ahead of them, also out of sight beyond a bend in the trail. Taylor felt the roan horse trembling under him. He could see Green's chestnut horse was nervous too, after cat-walking along this narrow trail. It wouldn't take much to spook either animal . . .

Green looped the rope around Taylor's wrists. He rested his pistol on the saddle but he didn't take his hand from the weapon. As he ran the end of the rope around the saddle horn, Taylor tugged gently against the pull of it. Green swore and said, 'Lean forward, damn you — '

Taylor spurred his horse. The animal screamed; it reared straight up. Green's horse reared also. As the rider was jerked back in the saddle, he lifted the pistol in his right hand. Taylor sprang. He got both of his hands to Green's right wrist, his right shoulder catching the man in the chest, lifting him in the saddle; for a crazy second both men stood in the stirrups, swaying, whilst their horses reared and pawed the air beneath them; then Green fell, and Taylor fell after him.

They struck on the edge of the trail. Green, underneath, cried out in pain. By chance, his knee had caught Taylor in the belly, half-winding him, but Taylor kept his grip on the man's right wrist. They struggled to their feet, strained together on the edge of a sheer drop. Behind them the horses scrabbled for footing on level ground, sending loose rocks and earth spilling downslope, raising dust. One of the horses screamed.

Green twisted suddenly, tripping his opponent. Taylor pitched headlong. Space opened beneath him and he swung out over the void, clinging to the other's wrists. Green jerked back, yanking him from the edge. Taylor kneed the other man in the ribs. Green gasped, doubling forward. Taylor used his knee again, catching

Green under the chin. Green snapped over, back arched inwards and fell, sprawling. Taylor discovered he was left with the Colt in his hand. Green was squirming on his side at the edge of the drop. He might have grabbed at the saddle horn of his horse, where his rifle was scabbarded. Instead, his right hand went down to the top of his boot and Taylor caught the flash of metal as the knife came from its hiding place. Green sat up, raising his right arm. He was sideways on to Taylor, who cocked the pistol and fired. Green was slammed back against the earth. He lay on his side, kicking.

Taylor ran over to Green's horse. He snatched the Winchester from the saddle scabbard as the animal whirled about, lashing out at him with a rear hoof. The kick missed; the horse bolted down the trail.

Taylor walked over to the fallen man. His shot had taken Green in the left cheek and exited through the other cheek, blowing away the right side of his face. Taylor tried not to look at that as he felt in the top pocket of the dead man's jacket. He found the long piece of wire and instantly he set to, trying to pick the lock on the handcuffs.

He looked up as his own horse whinnied. The animal had probably tried to bolt too, but had got its forefeet tangled in the reins. Beyond the horse, he glimpsed movement. Andersson came into view, getting as much speed as he could out of his grey horse on this narrow trail. He had a rifle in his hand.

Taylor had never fired a rifle whilst his wrists were handcuffed before; he didn't know if it could be done. He threw himself on his side. He found he could just get the weapon braced against his shoulder, at the same time pulling his left arm to full stretch. He supposed he looked ridiculous, but was too frightened to worry about that; any minute, Alva and Zale would come boiling out of the trees behind him and he'd be trapped between both sets of enemies. He rested the rifle on the dead man's chest. Andersson reined in his horse lifting his rifle to his shoulder; for that one instant he was a sitting target. Taylor shot him out of the saddle. Andersson fell on the edge of the trail. His horse spun about, galloping back the way it had come.

The range detective sat up, wincing with sudden pain. The recoil of the Winchester might have broken his shoulder. Making other pain-filled noises, he continued working on the handcuffs with the twist of wire. He got the right cuff unclipped, then hooves clattered on stones behind him, he turned and saw Alva, and then Zale, burst from the cover of the trees.

Taylor knew he ought to let these men get nearer, but his hands seemed to act ahead of his thinking, pulling the rifle into his injured shoulder and jerking the trigger. Through the dark burst of powdersmoke he saw Alva and Doc halting their horses, both men lifting pistols and firing. Taylor started to lever and fire the Winchester as fast as he could work the action. A horse squealed. Caught in the open, his enemies scattered like quail; they plunged back into the trees and he heard hooves hammering into distance.

Taylor's shoulder hurt fiercely but he guessed it was bruised, not broken. Alternately gasping and swearing at the pain, he got to his feet. He listened a minute for Alva and Zale's return. He heard nothing. Up the trail, Andersson lay sprawled out, his right arm pinned under him. Taylor's roan horse shifted forefeet tangled in the reins, making the tangling worse.

The range detective managed to unclip the other cuff from his wrist and spent a minute massaging the flesh where the metal bracelets had gripped. He walked over to Green, scavenging what he could from the dead man. He took rifle, pistol, cartridge belt and, for good measure, the long-bladed skinning knife Green had hidden in his boot.

He walked over to his horse, keeping Andersson in the tail of his eye. He bent and began to untangle the reins around the horse's feet. Half of his attention was on his back-trail; he watched to see if Zale and Alva would reappear. Then he realized something: Andersson had been lying on his right arm, now he lay sprawled on his *left*.

Taylor stood and turned; Andersson was pushing himself to his feet. His shirt and jacket were bloody, his face twisted in pain and anger. He lifted a pistol in his right hand. He came to full height. In his right hand, Taylor gripped the skinning knife by the blade; he threw the weapon putting all his strength into the throw. It turned four or five times in the air, then the bone hilt was standing out from Andersson's chest just above the heart. Andersson reeled. His pistol discharged but the shot went wide. Andersson opened his mouth and for a second, there was no sound, then he gave a terrible, rending cry. He staggered backwards, stepped back into space and fell straight down, seventy or eighty feet. He struck on a slope of boulders and jutting, broken rocks.

Taylor turned and saw his roan horse lying dead on the trail; Andersson's shot had caught the animal in the forehead. He stumbled over to the fallen horse and sat on the earth by it. He supposed if he had anything in his stomach to bring up, he would have vomited. A violent shaking took him. Andersson's dying cry came again and again in his head.

Eventually he moved. He stripped what he needed from the saddle of his horse. He walked eastward along the trail. He wasn't afraid of being set afoot in this country, he'd learned enough, from the Apaches and others, to survive, and there was a reliable water-hole, twelve or fifteen miles east, almost on the New Mexico line. He could make that today. He was more concerned about how he'd catch Alva and Zale.

He reached the place where Alva and Zale had burst from the trees, where they'd stood under his fire. He found spent cartridges on the earth.

And something else: a large patch of fresh blood.

20

Doc Zale said, 'Alva, I've got to stop.'

Alva nodded. He reined in his horse.

They were riding double. Zale's horse had caught a bullet in the skirmish with Taylor. The animal had made a few miles along the trail, bleeding copiously, before dropping dead. Now Zale hung against the mane of Alva's horse. Alva slipped from the saddle behind him glancing over his shoulder, at their back-trail. The wonder of it was that Taylor hadn't caught up with them yet.

It was an hour past noon. They'd dipped below the timber, coming down into high desert country. Coppery slopes stippled with giant cactus, a tortured, alien world, blurred with haze, under a coruscating sun.

Alva said, 'There's a water-hole, just up ahead.'

Zale couldn't find the breath to answer, he nodded. Alva felt his usual revulsion looking at Zale's exhausted, chalk-white face and bloody lips, listening to him. Doc still found enough poison in the ruin of his lungs to cough up. It occurred to Alva that Zale might not make it to the next settlement, he might not even last out the night. The rough travel of the last few days had just about broken him.

With Alva leading the horse, they reached the water-hole; a spring fed clear water into a square rock basin. It was a spot of green, timber, grama grass, on the scalded face of the land, with slopes rising fairly steeply behind, to orange cliffs. Beyond those cliffs was New Mexico. If they pushed east another mile, they'd be out of Arizona. But they needed to make this one last camp, men and horse needed water and rest. They drank.

Alva filled the canteens. He told Zale, 'Come on, Doc. We'll camp on the slope up there.' He nodded towards the rising ground east of the water-hole.

Zale managed to say, 'But Taylor . . . '

'We'll wait here for Taylor.' Alva took Zale's arm. 'We'll wait here and finish this.'

He led Zale to cover, then picketed the horse in some trees. He studied the land to the west, trying to see through the haze. Taylor ought to have been on them by now, maybe something had happened to his horse . . .

Thinking of Taylor, Alva felt his lips purse with anger. It was, directly or indirectly, because of the Wells Fargo man that all of Alva's plans had come out wrong, that Levi was dead, that he was now being hunted through this desolation, with only a dying man left to side him. He ought to be living like a king in Coffin Creek, with the whole county in his pocket. Instead he was cornered in this wilderness, brought to bay like a trapped animal. If only Doc had killed the right man in the stage hold-up, instead of Pike

Sandusky . . . but there was no profit in 'if onlys'.

Doc lay on his side, trying to breathe, his eyes closed. Alva glanced at him, then focused his attention on the water-hole below them. This wasn't his speciality; he wasn't a wild country hand, he'd lived too long in towns . . . but even Taylor had to drink, he'd have to come here for water. Then all Alva would need would be the one clear shot.

He checked his Winchester, trying to remember the last time he'd fired it; he'd got out of practice with long guns. He checked his pistol and counted the shells looped in his cartridge belt, the spares in his pocket. He had enough ammunition to fight a small-scale Mexican revolution, but all it needed was the one bullet in the right place . . . all he needed was to keep steady. *Stay steady*, just like he'd told Levi. As he thought about Levi, he knew hatred was making his face a mask. When he got his chance at

Taylor, he wouldn't miss.

After that, he'd shake the dust of Arizona from him for keeps. He'd take Zale to the nearest New Mexico settlement and leave him there. Later, if Doc was still alive, Alva would come back for him, take him to a sanatorium somewhere, Colorado say, where the cold, clear mountain air might repair his lungs. In the meantime, Alva would find another territory, somewhere he wasn't known, the Pacific north-west perhaps, and let his legend build anew; another place where, once this Arizona mess was forgotten, the pickings would be easy, ripe and luscious . . .

He'd been daydreaming. He came from his reverie suddenly. A dot was moving on the sun-bleached plain before him. It was a man afoot, coming towards this water-hole . . . Alva gripped his Winchester, he slid the brass-bound butt into his shoulder . . .

★ ★ ★

Taylor paused and squatted down. He studied the water-hole backed against the cliffs. His every instinct told him that Alva and Zale were there, hiding in the trees and long grass back of the tank. They couldn't have got much further, two men on one tired horse, and one of those men as sick as you could be and still be alive. So the water-hole was most probably a trap, and Alva had a rifle trained on him right now.

Taylor still had some water left in the canteen he'd scavenged from Green, but he needed more . . . the thought of it filled his mind. It would be green and warm and full of scum and floaters, but in his imagination, it tasted of ice, sharp, chill.

He moved forward. Alva was a city boy, he thought, how good would he be with a rifle, at fighting in this kind of country? It took something, sitting and waiting to fight . . . would Alva have the nerve for it?

The range detective decided he was

now inside rifle range. He halted and spent a few minutes studying the brushy slopes above the tank, seeing nothing. He glanced at the water and remembered how thirsty he was, but he decided to take care of business first, and drink afterwards. If he was still alive . . . He moved forward at an angle that would take him well clear of the water-hole, then struck a dim trail that bent into the cover above it, a tangle of tall grass, mesquite and chaparral, brush taller than a man in places. All at once he felt his patience running out, Andersson's scream was in his head, half of Green's face lay on the trail, heat, dust, thirst, fear, all of it was wearing at him. Suddenly he thought the hell with it, draw some lightning; he was probably scurrying around in the brush for no reason anyway, his enemies were probably long gone. He moved into the open. Nothing happened. Taylor felt tension ease out of him; he grinned foolishly, stepped forward and the shot came.

It struck him on his left side, about level with the bottom rib. He spun, went down on his back and rolled. He kept rolling until cover swallowed him. There was another shot, then a third, but he wasn't hit.

He lay still then, in the trapped head of the underbrush, whilst the blood pumped in his ears and pain ran along his side like fire. He was bleeding a fair amount, the blood had already soaked his side and his left leg, leaving him nauseous and dizzy. But he judged the wound wasn't serious, it had probably only skated over his ribs; it hurt too much to be a crippling wound. He told himself 'You stupid bastard!' Alva shouted; he recognized the man's voice but he couldn't make out the words. Alva tried another shot, but it didn't come close.

Taylor started to snake forward on his belly, being careful to keep his rifle out of the dust, which could foul the mechanism, and not wave the barrel. He hissed with pain as he crawled. Coming to the edge of cover, he crouched there, trying to summon the courage for what he had to do next, then broke into the open, running. He ran Apache-style, bent over, zigzagging. There were two shots, almost simultaneous, and then he was in more cover, ploughing to his knees, getting up and running on and going to ground behind a cluster of small boulders.

He was dizzy from loss of blood, soaked in his own sweat. He sleeved some of the sweat from his eyes and squinted ahead. The ground began to climb fairly steeply, there was less brush and more rocks and boulders. He couldn't see anyone; Alva was better at this game than he had supposed . . .

Taylor called, 'I'm going to kill you, Alva! You and Zale! You killed Dave McLennan! And Pete, and the Hooks! And Pike Sandusky!'

Alva made a strange noise. After a moment, Taylor recognized it as harsh laughter, then Alva shouted, 'But aren't you a servant of the law, Taylor? Just like me? That's it, ain't it? You're just like me!' He laughed again.

The range detective thought he had a rough fix on Alva's voice now, in cover about a hundred yards upslope. Taylor ran for the next bunch of rocks. Alva showed himself, lifting to fire. Taylor felt the wind of the bullet and he yelled with fear as he went down behind some shattered boulders. Once again, he sleeved away sweat. He was still bleeding; he thought: please God, don't let me pass out from loss of blood. If that happened, Alva would have the last laugh after all.

Another thing was troubling him. He realized he'd unconsciously discounted Zale from the fight, but you could be desperately sick and still pull the trigger. He had a flesh-crawling feeling that Zale was behind him, might even be levelling a gun on his back right now.

Whilst he was thinking about that, Alva showed himself again, firing, the bullet chipping the boulder in front of Taylor, driving shards of rock towards his face. Taylor fired back and the two men exchanged several shots. It must have been too hot for Alva for he turned and ran upslope. Taylor fired at his back, missed and saw Alva dodge behind a tall, slim boulder at the base of the cliff.

Taylor grinned woflishly; he'd backed his enemy against a wall. He studied the cliff face a moment, then fired at it. He heard the vicious whine of a ricochet.

Alva called, 'Henry!'

Taylor drove another shot at the cliff base, angling another ricochet into Alva's hiding place; then he fired again. Alva yelled and sprang clear of the boulder, out into the open. Taylor shot him. Alva fell sideways, dropping his rifle. Taylor moved from cover and he was halfway to the next rock when he saw Alva writhe off the ground, pulling his Smith and Wesson from his jacket pocket. Alva fired. The bullet struck the barrel of Taylor's rifle, twisting the weapon from his hands. Taylor grunted and slipped to one knee. He saw Alva struggle upright, his right shoulder bloody, and run downslope. Taylor found his right hand was numbed. With his left hand, he pulled the Colt from his holster, firing and missing. Alva sprang into the long grass and vanished.

Taylor spent a minute, flexing and kneading the fingers of his numbed hand until feeling returned to them. He gripped his pistol in his right hand, got to his feet and stepped forward. Behind him he heard a dry, racking cough. He turned. Zale lay in the shade of a few mesquite trees, lifting the pistol in his right hand. Taylor fired at Zale, flinging himself sideways, landing badly on shale and loose stones. Zale's pistol sounded, but Taylor felt no smashing impact. He raised himself up on one elbow and saw Zale aiming his pistol again; he had a bead on Taylor's chest. The man's face twisted, as if squeezing the trigger required a superhuman effort. Then he began to cough, he sank down, coughing into the back of his forearm, his shoulders heaving.

The other man stood. He glanced over at his rifle, seeing the bullet had twisted the barrel at a crazy angle. He fed shells into the pistol. He collected Alva's rifle, checking the loads in the magazine, then set off after him.

His quarry had vanished into a pocket of grass that grew taller than a man, moving slightly in the vaguest breeze. Taylor stepped through this green curtain. Suddenly he could see no further than a yard in any direction. He halted, listening. He heard nothing. But he saw, on the earth by his foot, a large gout of blood, and then more blood, edging the grass. He held still; there was a long silence.

Alva broke the silence, calling, 'Come and get me, you sonofabitch!' He fired a shot but it didn't come anywhere near his enemy; maybe his nerve had totally gone and he was firing blindly at anything. Under his breath, Taylor said, 'All right.'

He got down on his belly and began to crawl forward. He moved out of the cover of long grass into a tangle of cholla and mesquite; ahead of him was a boulder-strewn slope. Taylor crouched behind one fair-sized rock. He continued to pour sweat; tension clenched him like a fist and he knew this was when you could lose your head, go crazy, fire blindly, make one stupid, fatal mistake. He tried breathing regularly, to get himself under control. He felt his blood-soaked left side but the bleeding had stopped. He studied the boulders on the slope above him. One boulder particularly. There was a riot of brush behind this rock; could he see a dim shape standing behind the screen of foliage? He squinted to see better. A canyon wren sailed in, making for the same brush, but at the last minute the bird flared its wings, veered away. To himself, Taylor said, 'Got you.'

He eased forward, snaking between rocks, until he came to the foot of the boulder. Coming to a crouch, he began to move forward, rounding the right side of the giant stone. He levelled the Winchester. A few more steps, past the next angle of rock and he and Alva would be face to face . . .

Taylor stepped forward; he heard a whisper of sound. Some instinct made him turn as Alva rounded the left side of the boulder, coming up behind him! Taylor threw himself headlong, landing on his right shoulder. He heard Alva's pistol discharge, squirmed over, saw Alva lifting his pistol again. Taylor got the butt of the Winchester to his shoulder and fired. Alva was knocked sideways; he fell on his back but almost instantly knelt up, the pistol still in his hand.

Taylor stood. After a second, he decided he hadn't been hit again. He trained his rifle on Tengen's chest. Alva had been wounded in the shoulder, another bullet had torn his shirt on the left side. There was blood all over him, his black broadcloth suit was now bloody and fouled with dust, his hat was gone, his hair was awry; he bared his teeth, showing blood on his lips. Slowly, he began to lift the pistol in his hand.

Taylor said, 'Give it up, Alva.'

Alva stood. His grimace became a smile, showing his bloody teeth. He brought up his gun.

Taylor fired. The shot caught Alva in the left chest, half turned him. Taylor triggered again, the hammer punched an empty chamber. Alva was still on his feet; he lifted his pistol, levelled it on the other man. Taylor worked the Winchester lever — another empty! Alva seemed to take an inordinately long time aiming, as if this were the most important shot he would ever make. Then something happened to his face, a glaze seemed to pass over his eyes. He lifted his right foot as if to take another step forward, then he fell headlong, ploughing into the earth on his face.

Taylor stared at the dead man. Finally, he said, 'How's your legend, Alva?'

He walked back to Doc Zale who still lay under the mesquites, coughing and sucking for breath. Seeing Taylor approach, he glanced at his pistol lying on the earth in front of him, within reach. But he didn't make a play for the gun. Instead, after some gasping and swallowing, he said, 'Kill me!'

Taylor said, 'You've got enough artillery: kill yourself!'

'Kill me! I killed Pike Sandusky!'

'Why should I?'

Anger squeezed and convulsed Zale's thin, aged face. 'If you was a Christian man, you would!'

'Neither of us is that.'

Zale spat; then he coughed. He was coughing long strings of blood with his saliva, Taylor could see, blood of an unnatural brightness. Zale managed to say, 'God damn you!' He lay back, his eyes almost closed.

Taylor said, 'God's got nothing to do with it.'

Zale's eyes opened, they widened, had a crazed, beseeching look in them. With what was left of his voice he asked, 'Where's Alva? Alva!'

Taylor began to walk downslope, towards the water-hole. As he stepped past Zale, he dropped a few things on the earth. Zale watched Taylor disappear into the brush downslope, then he glared at the objects he'd dropped: a Smith and Wesson pistol, the long barrel decorated with engraved scrolls and other markings, and a deputy US Marshal's badge, a dull, six-pointed star.

THE END

We do hope that you have enjoyed reading this large print book.

Did you know that all of our titles are available for purchase?

We publish a wide range of high quality large print books including:

Romances, Mysteries, Classics
General Fiction
Non Fiction and Westerns

Special interest titles available in large print are:

The Little Oxford Dictionary
Music Book, Song Book
Hymn Book, Service Book

Also available from us courtesy of Oxford University Press:

Young Readers' Dictionary
(large print edition)
Young Readers' Thesaurus
(large print edition)

For further information or a free brochure, please contact us at:

Ulverscroft Large Print Books Ltd.,
The Green, Bradgate Road, Anstey,
Leicester, LE7 7FU, England.
Tel: (00 44) **0116 236 4325**
Fax: (00 44) **0116 234 0205**